Cover: Original Artwork by Niikah Hatfield

Kana's Vardo

-a novella-

Niikah Hatfield

*It was a time where there was nothing,
and yet nothing was everything…*

Prologue

She stared out across the empty fields, pulling her coat closer around her. The wind plucked at her skirt and teased tears from her eyes, and the hollow feeling in her heart echoed the vastness that surrounded her.

Too many times had she stood there; too many times had she left without feeling whole. And once again, the heavy weight of loneliness pressed close, she turned away.

Her worn boots found the well tread path back to the road. She bent her head against the world, hid herself within layers of cloth.

A shout of laughter echoed across the hills, and she turned. The thump of hooves met her ears at the same moment she saw the vardos. Sleek horses drew the elaborate wagons, creaking as they rolled over the divots in the road. Barefoot children ran laughing among the turning wheels.

She watched with wide eyes as they rolled past where she stood: men with dark hair and skin, women in colorful skirts. They watched her, but no one met her gaze accept one, a woman with stunning long locks and a glowing face.

She felt drawn to her the moment their eyes met; saw the mysteries behind her eyes. She stared for a moment longer than she should have. A wide smile drew across the woman's face, and then she looked away.

The moment was gone.

Chapter 1

She walked up the path to their small hut, built a little farther away from the rest. She stooped, lifting the heavy basket of dirty wash she had collected earlier and pushed the door open with her hip.

"Sade."

She looked up as she closed the door behind her. Her father's face was gaunt in the firelight. His eyes looked duller than usual, his body frailer than before.

"Where have you been?" His voice rasped.

Sade hung her coat on the hook beside the door and let the basket fall with a thump on the floor. The fire burst up as she put another log on the burning coals, and she spread her hands towards the warmth.

"I went for a walk."

He shifted in his chair, the whicker creaking like his old bones.

"You worry me, child. You shouldn't be out alone at night, wandering around like a lost man."

Sade took his hands in hers.

"I am fine, Papa," she whispered, kissing him on the brow.

She left him sitting there by the fire and crawled under the layers of blankets on her bed. As she watched his silhouette flicker in the firelight, a quiet sadness washed over her. What did he think about, these nights when he stayed up by the fire?

Maybe, she thought, *he is as sad as I, if only in a different way.*

She closed her eyes; remembered the look of the Gypsy woman. She tried to find, in the spinning turmoil inside her, the feeling of peace that she felt when she had met the woman's eyes.

It was the same look, she though, that Nemea had often given her. Happy, welcoming, mysterious. Memories of evenings spent in laughter beside her fireplace and long walks through the woods swept her up, and tears dropped down onto the sheets. She remembered the old woman's smile that always gleamed when she taught Sade her secrets. Forgotten laughter echoed in her ears as she fell asleep, lost in the tunnels of darkness.

A cry awoke her feverish in the night. She lay in the darkness, listening with wide eyes. There was no sound, and slowly she felt her tense muscles relax. Blue moonlight fell through the window onto the floor; the fire glowed in embers.

Sade curled up under her blankets, but she could not fall back asleep. She listened to the wheeze of her father; the distant bark of a dog somewhere in the night.

Restless, she slipped out of bed and pulled on a coat and her worn leather shoes. The door closed with a soft thud behind her as she walked down the road towards the hill. Everything was bathed in moonlight, and the landscape seemed quiet and serene. The cool air cleared her mind, and she closed her eyes.

For a moment, she thought she heard something—a song, maybe. But when she opened her eyes, it was gone, and there was only the whispering breeze in the grass.

Puzzled, she wandered down the road, away from all the houses.

There it came again—louder, this time.

She was wide awake, then. She hugged her arms to herself and took off through the grass. The breeze brought the sound of music to her ears, intermingled with laughter.

Her breath caught in her throat as she rounded the crest of a hill. Spread out below her was the kumpania, light spilling from the fires and dancing on the vardos. Silhouettes of figures moved among them, and beyond that, the dusky shapes of the horses.

Curiosity ran through Sade's bloodstream, urging her to go closer. Her heart thumped at the wild daring of it all, but she still went among the waving grass. Bright splashes of color solidified into women dancers, the hunkering shapes beside them musicians.

She stood beyond the shadows and watched, wonder growing in her throat. She had never seen dancers like that before. Their movements were careless and free, yet something about it was still graceful and quiet and beautiful.

For a long while she stood there and watched. She was brought back to the moment only when the music stopped. One of the women bent and kissed a man, and she turned away, suddenly unable to watch any more.

Chapter 2

"Sade?"

Her father was sitting looking out the window. He didn't look at her as he spoke; his eyes seemed lost in the distance.

"The Romani are here."

She caught her breath, fearing he knew she had left in the night, but when she realized he wasn't looking at her, she let out the breath like a heavy sigh.

"I know." She scrubbed the sheets harder against the washboard.

She felt his gaze on her back. "You know?"

"I saw them last night, before I came home." The water splashed against the sides of the basin as she started work on a table linen.

"Why didn't you tell me?"

Sade shrugged. "I didn't think it was important."

Her father shifted in his seat, running a hand through his graying hair. He let out a deep breath. "Some people will tell you that the Romanies will steal without mercy, Sade, but it isn't true. They really are kind people—they just see us as being susceptible to their cleverness."

Sade stood up, piling the washing into a basket. She paused, then, and looked at him.

"Why are you telling me this?"

He sighed. "I just wanted you to know."

He pulled himself to his feet, slowly putting on his jacket. Sade watched him with a raised eyebrow.

"I'm going out," he said matter-of-factly.

Sade raised her eyebrows as he closed the door, leaving her in silence. Sun glittered from a cloudless sky, and a warm breeze plucked at fine strands of her hair as she hung the laundry to dry on the ropes stretching from the house to distant poles.

Even after she had gone back inside, her mind kept turning to the Gypsies and her father's abruptness. The look on his face when he had spoken of the Romani was the same as when he spoke of her mother. Distant, hesitant, and almost wishful.

The sun dipped lower in the sky, and when he didn't come back, Sade went outside, telling herself that she would take the laundry down and bring it back to her clients. Yet her footsteps led her past the blowing cloth, down the path towards the Gypsy camp.

She didn't know what she would find there — maybe there would be nothing. Maybe they would already be gone, and she would never see them again.

She told herself fiercely that it didn't matter, but still her heart rose when she saw the tops of the vardos appear over the hill. She didn't dare go closer this time, without the safety of darkness to hide her.

A handful of heads could be seen bobbing through the grass; children as they played. The men and women around the kumpania were busy, too. It looked as if everyone had their own task, and yet through their work a thread of talk and laughter drifted up to Sade.

They seem so happy, she thought.

"You like our people?"

Sade jumped and spun around. She found herself face to face with the Gypsy woman from the day before.

She took a step backwards in surprise, embarrassed to be caught watching them. "I…"

The woman smiled, wrinkles forming in the corners of her dark eyes.

"It's all right."

She spoke with a heavy accent and a sparkle in her eye. Her dark hair was looped up under a red scarf, and she wore a simple rust shirt tucked into a brown skirt. She appeared ageless, and Sade got the intense feeling that she was looking at someone who had never been born and who would never die.

The woman stood beside Sade and looked down with her at the kumpania.

"You remind me of someone I once knew," she remarked, catching Sade's gaze again. She reached out and touched her hair, very gently. "You are sad, though, are you not?"

Sade caught her breath; stepped away from her touch.

"I…I should go now," she muttered, turning away. Her heart thumped in her chest; she didn't dare look back. She could feel the woman's gaze follow her away, but she didn't turn to face it. Something deep within her had shifted, pierced by the arrow of her words.

You are sad, are you not?

Only once the door of her home was closed firmly behind her did she breath easily again. Shaken, she took up the broom and concentrated on sweeping the floor. She tried to push the encounter out of her mind and sweep it away with the dust, but when she paused for a moment too long it was blaring at the front of her mind.

It shouldn't matter, she thought. *She simply knew that I was sad.*

Still, it startled her, somehow. There were stories of Romani woman telling fortunes. She had never believed them, but there was something in the woman's eyes, something so sincere.

Sade shook her head and went on, moving from one moment to the next. She folded the laundry, put on a pot of stew from the night before, began to wonder where her father was. The Romani woman was pushed out of her mind as the dark deepened. By the time the day grew dim as the sun set behind the trees, he still had not come.

Where had he gotten to? He never went out—not this late.

She took the pot off the fire and wrapped the bread to keep it warm. She tried to read one of the few books that she owned, but the words only swam before her eyes.

Finally, she got up and pulled a shawl around her shoulders. Just as she bent to blow out the candle, the door creaked and swung open.

"Papa!" Sade cried out as he stumbled inside.

She grabbed his arm as he stood there swaying uncertainly, his eyes glazing over. Drool seeped out of the corner of his mouth. His jacket was twisted on his shoulders, and in his hand he clung to an empty bottle.

"What happened to you?" Sade whispered, guiding him to his chair, wiping away the spittle and prying the bottle from his grasping hold.

He blinked, and his head rolled.

"Come." She coaxed him to his bed, taking off his coat and boots. He gazed up at her as she drew a blanket over him, yet not a word passed his mouth. She tried to get him to drink some water, but he turned his head away.

Her heart thumped as she filled a bowl of food for him.

"Here, Papa," she said, sitting down beside him.

She held out a spoon of glistening broth, but he shook his head and rolled away from her. She sat there for a moment, staring bewilderingly at him.

"What happened to you?"

Watching his chest rise and fall in a fitful sleep, she ate by herself. She wondered what had made him drink: he hadn't touched the bottle in as long as she could remember.

Swaying in the rocking chair, she became lost in the remains of the fire. The floor creaked every time the rocker passed over a loose board, but beyond that there was silence. Her mind drifted again to the Gypsy woman. Sade felt struck by how the woman had pin-pointed her feelings, but at the same time was wary at how right she had been.

A heavy feeling settled deep in her stomach, a small knot of dread. She stepped outside for a moment and took a deep breath. In the near distance she could hear the feint ringing of Gypsy music. She listened for a moment as it ebbed in and out of her hearing range, and then turned back inside.

Chapter 3

"Papa? Are you alright?"

Sade went to him as he struggled to sit up in his bed. His hair was tossed in a wild mess, and deep circles ran around his eyes. He looked at Sade, closed his eyes, and took a shuttering breath.

"Papa? Jo!"

His name came out as a cry as she reached out and laid a hand on his arm.

He patted her hand. "I'm fine, darling, I am fine."

He rubbed his face, pressing his fingers to his temples. With a shaky hand, he smoothed down his hair; one stubborn cowlick refused to lay flat.

He looks so tired, Sade thought. *Worn; suddenly years older than he was before*.

"Sade... some water," he croaked.

Sade took a cup down from the shelf and dipped the ladle into the bucket. His eyes glistened as she bent over him and held the ladle out to him. When he drank, drops of water dribbled down his chin and splashed on his shirt.

She sat down beside him, her hand resting on his arm.

"Why did you do this to yourself?"

He sighed a heavy sigh, gripping the edge of the bed and letting his head fall to his chest. His eyes closed, and he sat there, a pure picture of a defeated man.

"You mustn't go to the Gypsies," he whispered

Sade's arm dropped in surprise. "What?"

He met her eyes, and the muscles in his cheeks grew taught.

"You mustn't go to the Gypsies," he repeated.

Sade sucked in a breath. Did he know that she had gone to watch them?

"Papa...," she shook her head. "I don't understand. Why...?"

He gripped her arm, his fingers digging into her. "You can't let them know who you are. Do you hear me?"

Sade pulled away, her eyes wide as she distanced herself from this suddenly fierce man. His stare was penetrating; it made her want to go run and hide. He seemed tense — angry, even.

"Did you hear me, Sade?"

Sade rubbed her arm where he had gripped her, her eyes darting away.

"Yes, I heard you," she whispered.

"So you won't go, then?"

Tears formed in the corners of Sade's eyes, more because she was afraid than angry. She couldn't understand—he had never, not once in her life, demanded something like this of her. He had been firm plenty of times, but never had he shown this angry side. She looked away.

"I won't go. I promise."

Almost instantly, he slumped over, his head in his hands. All sign of anger left.

"I'm sorry." He reached out a frail hand, as if to draw back the words he had said and pull Sade towards himself again. But she turned away, the door thudding closed behind her.

Sade held her arms to her chest as she walked away. It was cool, but she didn't dare go back for her coat. She turned towards the empty hills, her feet following the secret path that she had walked so many times. Eyes closed, she breathed deeply the sweet smell of grass and tilted her head towards the sky.

The sound of crickets met her ears. Their song was simple, ever present, humming with the first breath of summer. Overhead, the cry of a meadow lark lingered soft and sweet in the still air.

She walked on, leaving all thoughts of her father behind her. She avoided the Romani camp. Her father, in those words, had instilled a sudden fear of the people; the very people whom he had told her the day before were kind and not what most folks thought of them.

Up on the hill, *her* hill, as she had come to think of it, she sat down and drew her legs up to her chest. Resting her chin on her knees, she looked out, watching the lark dip down into the waving grass. Her eyes followed its flight to where it disappeared into the forest beyond.

She wanted to curl up in a hidden place and fall asleep forever. She didn't want to face this, the unrest she now felt spiraling into her life.

"Nemea?"

The name fluttered on her lips, a question ringing out into the emptiness. No reply came, only the wind on her cheek. Her fingers traced careless circles in the dirt. She tried to remember what it felt like the last time Nemea had embraced her, but her memories only came up with empty air.

Why wasn't life simple anymore? Why couldn't she still be the careless young girl she once was, when her only thought was to pick the next flower she saw or climb upon her father's back?

She lay back in the grass, her eyes a reflection of the evening sky. As slowly as the clouds shifted across the sky, she felt the cold creeping into her body, turning her feelings numb. The turmoil within her began to settle, until she could breathe easily once more. She lay there in the whispering silence until dusk began to fall and the horizon became pink with the light of the setting sun. With the fading light it grew cooler, and she wrapped her arms around herself.

A sense of inner peace filled her as she pulled herself slowly to her feet. She took a deep breath, looking out once more at the serenity that lay around her before tearing herself away.

By the time she reached their hut, she felt a rising sense of dread at the thought of facing her father. It displaced the calm she had felt, and her hand trembled when she reached for the handle and pushed the door open.

He was sitting in his chair, looking out the window. He looked at her as she came in, but she avoided his gaze. In the burning silence, Sade took off her boots and set them beside the door. Then she moved across the floor and carefully filled her cup with water and drank.

"I am sorry," he said.

Sade took in a shallow breath, but she didn't look at him. She wrestled with her growing anger and tried to restore the calm feeling she had been enveloped in up on the hill.

He got up, the floorboards creaking as he came and stood behind her. She could feel his breath on her shoulder as he seemed to hesitate. She concentrated on peeling the onion before her.

"I never should have said what I did."

From the onion or emotion, Sade didn't know, but tears formed in the corner of her eyes. She turned to face him, the food still in her hand.

"Why did you, then?" She asked softly.

She saw the pained look that flashed across his face as he turned away. He didn't say anything, and she wiped her eyes with her sleeve and turned back to the cutting board. Taking a deep breath, she composed herself.

"I…" He began.

"Can we just let it go?" She whispered, clenching her jaw.

She heard him let out a heavy sigh. He stood there for a moment longer, and then he went to the door. Sade looked up in sudden worry as he put his hat on, but he shook his head.

"I won't touch the bottle." His hand rested on the handle, and he paused. "I love you, Sade," he said before going out the door.

Sade closed her eyes in the moment of silence that followed, and let out a breath she hadn't known she was holding. The words echoing in her mind, she bent once more towards her work.

Chapter 4

Twice more, the sun crossed the sky, the days passing quietly and without notice. Her father was more or less as he had been before, but there was still an aura of silence that surrounded him. Sade felt like every second of the day she thought of how he had been, and intermingling with those memories were thoughts of the Gypsy woman.

She tried to put it behind her, to forget what had happened.

Maybe, she thought, *it was just a momentary sense of panic that had brought him to drink. Maybe he wasn't quite in his mind when he had grown so stern.*

She told this to herself over and over again, but in the bottom of her heart she knew that it wasn't the case. She felt the distance growing between them as she watched. She saw how tired he was.

They sat together before the fire, their stomachs full with supper. Sade looked at his slumping form, suddenly shifting her gaze back to the fire when he tried to catch her eyes. The embers pulsed like glowing orbs, and the fire danced along the logs. She was reminded, suddenly, of the Romani dancers. Bright, there, and gone again.

She took a deep breath. "What made you drink?"

He let out a nasal sigh. When she looked at him, he was rubbing his face with his hands. The lines of his face seemed etched with sadness, and his face no longer seemed to glow.

There was a long silence that followed. Finally, and without a word, he stood up and went to bed. He left his clothes in a pile on the floor. Sade watched him climb beneath the blankets, waiting for him to answer her. After a while of listening to him toss and turn, she realized that he wasn't going to say anything.

It wasn't long before the sounds of his snoring filled the room. Sade stood up and pulled on a shawl, staring for a moment at his sleeping form. Her heart thumped in her chest, her hand resting on the door handle. Even before the door closed behind her, she knew she was going to go to the Romani camp.

The waxing moon lit her path; the sky above was filled with a thousand pinpricks of brightness. She didn't notice, though. Her head was bent towards the ground. She paused, for a brief moment, on the hill above the kumpania, taking a breath to compose herself.

She remembered the first time she ran across these hills as a young child, full of the wild feeling of freedom as she sprinted away from her father. She had never known a mother, but he had always been there for her. Yet when she cast a glance over her shoulder, she knew that there were some things that he couldn't understand.

She saw the Gypsy woman sitting beyond the fire, her face lit with brightness. Sade stared at the two thick braids falling over the woman's shoulders, and she hesitated at the edge of the ring of shadows. She trembled at the open disobedience to her father. And yet when she thought of going back, without knowing the woman's name and without settling the feeling of questioning in her heart, she felt even emptier than before.

The Romani watched her with wary surprise when she stepped from the darkness. She stood just within the ring of firelight, suddenly self-conscious and afraid. Their looks were not unkind, but there was no open welcome among them.

Words became jumbled in her mouth and heat rose in her cheeks. She realized, too late, that she had intruded on their personal space. She ducked her head, as if in apology, kicking herself in shame as she turned to leave. The woman stood up, stopping her, and under the watchful eyes of her companions came to Sade.

"T'aves mansa," she said, touching Sade's sleeve. "Come with me."

The woman led her away from the kumpania. She stopped well beyond the range of earshot and turned to Sade.

"Why did you come to us?" Her voice was soft, but still it was stern.

Sade met her eyes only for a moment, and then looked away at her feet. What she meant to put in words suddenly seemed trivial, and they stalled on the tip of her tongue.

When Sade didn't speak, the Gypsy tugged at a coin sewn into her hair.

"My name is Kana," she said.

It gave Sade the courage to look up, and she met the woman's gaze. "I'm Sade."

Kana nodded, as if she had already known, and smiled.

"I..." Sade wrapped her coat closer around her. Then the words rushed from her tongue before she could think twice about them. "How did you know I was sad?"

The Gypsy woman smiled in amusement, turning her face towards the stars.

"It is not hard to tell a person's emotions, if you know how to pay attention." She reached out and coaxed a stem of grass out of its sleeve, and put the sweet white part into her mouth. The seed head bobbed as she chewed on the end.

"You seem to be missing something," she remarked.

Her stark words brought tears to Sade's eyes. "Yes," she whispered, looking up to the sky.

"Do you want to share?"

"I—" She suddenly burst into tears, quiet tears that slid down her cheeks. "I don't know," she whispered hoarsely.

Kana's hand brushed away the wetness. "It is all right. You don't have to tell me."

Sade almost protested; she was burning to tell someone her sorrow, but already the moment was passed. Kana's hand slid to the small of her waist, and she was guided back to the kumpania. She whispered in Sade's ear that they would play a song for her, before she went home.

So she found herself sitting wrapped in blankets by the fire, the sole audience of a Gypsy band. They played a winding song, and Kana lifted her head to the stars and sang.

Sade listened, watching the fire dance, letting the moment infiltrate her being. At that moment, she didn't feel like a strange intruder into someone else's life. Instead, she felt oddly welcomed, as if she had always been meant to be there. She was afraid for the song to end, that it might shatter the fragile feeling in her heart.

She looked at the Gypsies in a new light; the innocent children sprawled asleep in their parents laps; the adults with happy and serene faces. Everyone seemed connected; peaceful. She suddenly was confused at why nobody liked the Gypsies; they seemed to her only harmless quiet people, choosing to live their lives away from the squalls of civilization.

She stood as the last notes of the song died away in the night. Kana smiled, her eyes glittering in the firelight.

"I'm glad to have met you, Sade," she said, holding out her arms to embrace her.

Sade bade her goodnight, turning away to hide the tears of joy in her eyes. She wandered back across the fields, a new sense of love and peace settling in her heart, and for the first time in a long while she looked up at the sky and really saw the stars shimmering in the night.

Chapter 5

Already the moon was waning when she returned again to their fire. Her heart thumped as she neared the twilight shadows, but Kana welcomed her with a strong embrace.

"Sade! I am so glad you have come," she whispered into her ear.

Kana led her to sit beside the others. She sat on the lap of a man, kissed him, and turned to Sade. "This is my husband, Van," she said. "Van, this is Sade."

He tipped his hat, grinning, but he didn't say anything. After a while, they began to play music. Kana begged Sade to join the dancers, but everyone just laughed with her when she refused to dance. They went on themselves, twirling sparks of light in the night. A toddler boy crawled into Sade's lap and fell asleep.

She sighed, laying her lips on the boy's soft head, the firelight dancing in her eyes. She dared not think of what would happen to this bubble of happiness when the kumpania went on its way again.

Her eyes followed each of the Romani in awe, trying to remember their gestures and figures of speech. She watched, wanting to be like them, and by the end of the night she shook her hair loose and smiled.

A young mother came and took the boy, and Kana sat down beside her. Her hair gleamed in the firelight, and her silver bracelets glinted. Her laugh was hearty and full, and there was softness in her eyes as she spoke.

"You remind me of someone, Sade."

"I know. You told me."

"Hmmm."

Then Sade cocked her head. "Who *do* I remind you of?"

"Me. When I was younger." She looked at Sade with a childish sort of grin.

They sat watching a strong black steed crop the grass.

"I used to ride a konja like that," she said to Sade. "Before it became unwomanly to lift my skirts above my knees. I would ride wildly across the fields…" She drifted off, watching the horse.

"Data never minded," she said softly, "but after he left the elders strictly forbade it. Even though Moma…" Kana paused, shaking her head. "But no matter about my lost memories."

"Your people love horses, no?"

Kana snorted. "A Romani man is nothing without his horse, Sade. They are our livelihood. We train them, and then trade them with those who are willing to do business with us."

Sade frowned. "Those who are willing?"

"The…common folk… aren't always welcoming to our people. The only time we really get to trade freely is at the Bromberg Fair. The Romani come together, leaving our differences behind, and the commoners come too." She sighed. "It is a wonderful time."

"Where is it?"

Kana gestured to the west, her hand fluttering indistinctively. "A good trek down this road. It's on the outskirts of Bromberg town, beside the Levine River."

Sade stared off into the distance where Kana pointed, drawing her knees up under her chin and dreaming of a festival where Gypsies danced and spoke freely with the 'commoners'. She imagined herself riding in a field beside Kana, laughing.

Kana's hand on her arm broke through her thoughts. "Do you want some tea?"

Sade nodded, pleasantly surprised at the offer. Kana led her to her vardo, and left her sitting on the steps while she went inside. After a moment she appeared again, holding two steaming cups. They sat side by side, sipping the sweet and tangy drink.

Sade took a deep breath, glancing at the woman beside her. "When you first saw me, you said that I was sad."

Kana nodded, plucking at the hem of her sleeve, waiting for Sade to go on.

"There was a woman, who lived in those woods." Sade gestured to the looming darkness in the distance. "Her name was Nemea. She was really old, and she lived all alone. I met her when I was eleven; maybe twelve. I had been running in the woods, and I found her hut. She scared me at first. Living all alone like that… I thought she was a bad woman, I think, because I had never met anyone like her."

Somewhere in the distance an owl hooted, and was answered a moment later by its mate.

"I loved her, Kana, even if she was different. I spent a lot of time with her; she taught me so much." Sade took a deep breath. "Last fall, she died."

She bit the inside of her cheek to quell the tears welling in her eyes. She looked up at the sky. The grief was still raw in her heart, but there was something comforting in telling someone.

Kana draped her arm around her. Sade expected her to say something, but she realized a moment later that silence was an even better cure than empty words. She closed her eyes.

"Thank you for listening, Kana," she whispered.

The woman smiled and squeezed Sade. "If there is anything I can do..."

Sade shook her head.

"I should go," she said, wiping away her tears with her sleeve. She wanted to stay longer, but she knew that she stretched her luck every moment she was gone.

"I have to go," Sade said again, stepping down the steps.

Kana reached out to take her hand. "I'm sorry about Nemea." Then she stood and hugged her, kissing her lightly on both cheeks.

"Goodnight, Sade."

She nodded at Kana in way of parting, and set off through the grass. When she paused and looked back, the Gypsy was shutting her vardo door behind her.

Sade lifted her head to the sky, closed her eyes, breathed in the fresh night air. For the first time since Nemea had died, she felt her mind clear. It was as if she had lovingly cut the thread that had bound her to the woman's memory, as if she at last let her spirit go into the ether.

Chapter 6

The laughter of Romani children drifted up the hills to the house, where Sade was pinning sheets to the drying lines. She looked up at one moment, and saw two young boys watching her from the bushes. When she smiled at them, they scampered away, and she shook her head with a grin.

Even though she stood still, her heart was thumping. Just the thought of Kana and the other Romani made her want to jump up and down like a little child.

Her mind drifted off with the breeze, swooping down the rolling valley to the kumpania. The dark skirt she wore gave way to a bright dress, and then she was riding beside Kana on their way to the Bromberg Fair.

"Sade!"

Her father's voice broke through her thoughts, and she spun around. She gripped the bed sheet in her hands, feeling guilty of her thoughts.

"What is it?" She asked, forcing her arms to slowly pin up the sheet.

"Mrs. McGowan said the Romani took grain from her husband's mill." His face was hard.

Sade bent down for another sheet, hiding behind it as she pinned it up. "What does that matter?" She saw his shadow shift behind the cloth.

"You haven't visited them, have you?"

Sade's hands stilled for a moment, and she tried to quell their shaking. "I haven't," she said evenly.

The sound of her father's shuffling feet. "If anyone sees you, they will dub you a traitor. They will drive you out with the rest of them."

Slowly, Sade picked up her empty basket and rested it on her hip, coming out from behind the fluttering cloth. "I told you; I have not gone," she said in a low voice, her eyes on the ground.

She felt her father's gaze on her for a long moment, and she let out a heavy sigh when he grumbled and closed the door behind him.

She lay awake for a long time that night, tossing and turning, wondering whether she should go and warn the Romani. She was afraid, yes. Especially after what he had said. But to lie there, knowing that at any time they could be gone, made her shiver.

The Romani fires had burned away to coals when she arrived, and there were only a few figures left beside them. She felt relief flood over her when she saw that one of them was Kana.

"I didn't expect to see you so late," Kana smiled, standing up to embrace her.

"I had to come," she said. "Papa said that the villagers will drive you out. That one of the Romani took grain from the McGowan mill."

Kana shook her head softly, gesturing for Sade to sit down beside her.

"The villagers will always drive us away, Sade. No matter what town, no matter what we have or haven't done. It is just the way of things, now." She reached out to touch Sade's arm when she saw her frown. "I am glad you thought to warn us, Sade, but you must know that it comes as no surprise."

"You won't go, then?" Sade asked, half hoping, half afraid.

Kana shook her head. "Not yet."

Sade stood up, suddenly confused and hurt. Kana grabbed the folds of her skirt, stopping her for a moment.

"We didn't take the grain, Sade."

Sade stared into the woman's eyes, afraid to believe anything now. She shook her head and pulled away. Her hands clutched the shawl around her shoulders as she walked back up the hill. She didn't stop to look back. Her mind was a jumble of twisting confusion, and she felt that one of the threads connecting her to Kana had just broken.

She barely realized until she shut the door that her father was watching her. She gulped, leaned back against it. Her heart pounded.

His eyes flashed in the firelight; the muscles that lined his jaw were tight. Slowly, Sade took off her coat and hung it on the hook.

"It's awfully late to be out, Sade."

She turned to face him, but didn't dare meet his eyes. She heard him shift, a board creaking underfoot. A heavy sigh.

"I asked one thing of you, Sade, and you disobeyed me." The last words were sharp, stinging as they hit.

"I—" Sade could think of nothing; her mind was suddenly blank. She wrapped her arms around herself and looked away, afraid that he would grow angry like before.

"Why didn't you stay away from them?" His voice hardened.

She covered her face with her hands and sank down on her bed.

"I'm sorry," she muffled.

"What?"

"I'm sorry!" She raised her eyes to him, to meet the whirling torment of his gaze. "I went to tell them to go," she said, tears pooling in her eyes. "To leave, before the townspeople turned on them. Is that so bad?"

His nostrils flared, and he ran a hand through his wild hair. He reached for a chair and lowered himself down. His head hung down, the veins pulsing in his neck.

"I just—" Sade looked out the window, wrestling the words that swirled within her. "They are the first people who have accepted me, Papa. I just don't understand why you don't want me to be with them."

"I told you to stay away, and you promised," he said in a low voice. "You lied to me!"

Fresh tears ran down Sade's cheeks; she looked at her hands lying clasped in her lap. His words punctured the silver bubble she had been in, and she felt the air deflating out of her as she sat under his stern gaze.

Chapter 7

The moment she awoke, the argument lay heavy on her mind. She left before her father got up and avoided him as the day went on. She felt, when they were together, that he was trying to redeem himself, but her raw anger made her turn away from his efforts.

He said nothing when he saw her looking wistfully out across the hills in the direction of the kumpania. She realized how much she had grown to love the Romani now that she was denied their company. She felt the longing to be with them grow beyond her control, yet she didn't dare to disobey her father again.

Yet why, in the end, did it matter to him?

She tried to remember any reason why he would hate the Gypsies, but the only thing that returned to her was when he told her that they were not like what people said. The more she tried to make sense of it, the more confusing it all became, and she fell asleep that night worse off than before.

Tossing and turning, she awoke in the night, hot under the layers of blankets. She kicked off the top two and lay back on her pillow. Her body was wide awake, and she felt an intense longing to walk out and find the Romani once more. Her gaze shifted to her father's sleeping form, the nasal snore, and she curled up again, knowing in her heart that she couldn't bring herself to go.

Chapter 8

The well was a bustle that morning as the women gathered to pull up buckets of water for their daily tasks. Sade elbowed her way forward and hooked her bucket to the rope, resting her head on the beam as the wheels turned to lower it down. With a distant splash she heard it hit the surface of the water, and she grabbed the handle and began to haul it back up.

All around her, gossip flew from mouth to mouth as the women waited for their turn. For the most part, she tried to ignore their senseless rumors, but the word *Gypsy* made her pause. A middle aged woman behind her was talking to her young consort, her head bobbing as she spoke.

"I won't have to lock my doors, now, either, that those ragamuffin Gyps are leaving," she huffed. "I heard they stole two of Steiner's chickens."

Sade gulped. "They are leaving, you say?" she asked.

The woman gave her a sidelong glance, nodding warily before turning her body away. Eyes wide, Sade took off at a half trot, the water sloshing against her skirts. Her hem was sopping wet when she reached her house. She left the bucket standing beside the door, her heart racing as she ran down the path towards the kumpania.

Please don't let them be gone, she prayed.

She didn't even think twice about what her father would say. It didn't matter, did it? If she saw Kana one more time? It almost brought tears to her eyes to think that she might already be gone, without words or a goodbye.

Her heart fluttered in relief when the vardo rooftops appeared over the crest of the hill. The caravan was packed up, some with horses already hitched and waiting. Her eyes ran wildly among the people until she saw Kana bending beside her wagon.

"Kana!" She cried, running the last paces down the hill.

"Sade!" she said, standing up. "It's been so long."

"I know, I'm sorry. I wasn't supposed to come." She reached out and hugged her. "You are leaving?"

The woman nodded, a sorrowful smile on her face. "It is time for us to move on."

"Where are you going?"

Kana shrugged. "Whatever road takes us to the Bromberg Fair."

Their eyes met.

"It is only a farewell," Kana whispered.

"I know. It's just that—" Sade hesitated, and then threw her arms around Kana again. "You have made me so happy."

Kana squeezed her.

"I am glad." She took Sade's face in her hands. "You are coming into yourself, Sade."

Sade looked at the ground, wiped away the dampness in her eyes. There grew a moment of silence, and her heartbeat quickened. Dare she ask what came on her mind? Her breathing was shallow. She looked up at Kana, seeing her as if for the first time. Beautiful, in her own exotic way; powerful; strong. So much *herself*.

Sade sucked in a breath. "I want to come with you."

Slowly, Kana shook her head.

"It can't be, Sade. I'm sorry." Kana touched her hair. "We will meet again when the time is right, but right now your place is here with Jo."

She was startled at the sound of her father's name. "Wha—"

Kana bent forward and kissed Sade on her brow, stilling the question on her tongue.

"Farewell, sister." She climbed up into the seat of her vardo beside Van, tipped her had to Sade, and then they were gone, too quickly for Sade to call out after them, too quickly for her to feel the sinking in her heart.

Chapter 9

Sade didn't know, then, what an impact those words made on her life. She returned to what she had been doing before the Gypsies had come: working, washing the town's laundry, caring for her father. Yet all too often, she found herself looking out over the fields, wondering where Kana might be.

So many hours, she spent, trying to put meaning to her last words. In no way could she understand how Kana had known her father's name, much less after he had told her not to tell the Romani who she was.

Unless, perhaps, Kana had met him in the streets, and he had somehow gotten in a quarrel with her or Van. Sade came to believe, without really knowing why, that that was what had happened. It made sense, in her mind, that he had then gotten drunk to forget it. He was a peaceful man, and maybe he didn't want to remember a shortcoming with a Gypsy.

She regretted the change that had come between them. Eventually their anger was forgotten, yes, but never again did they quite speak the same to each other. Even in the evenings when it was just them, or in a special moment when he brought her something from the market, some degree of wariness separated them.

The lunar cycles passed, and one day Sade came home from her rounds of gathering laundry to find her father pale in bed. She gasped, the baskets of dirty linens smacking the floor as she rushed to his bedside.

"Papa!"

He turned his sunken eyes to look at her, sweat glistening on his brow. He coughed, a hacking wheeze that sounded capable of a dying man. Sade rested a hand on his burning forehead.

"Let me make you some tea," she said, but he shook his head.

"I—" He coughed again, lay back on the pillow. He waved her away. "I am fine."

Sade shook her head, quietly lighting a fire and putting a kettle among the coals. She made him drink an herbal brew, and for a while the cough was gone.

She knelt on the floor, then, washing the linens in a big tub and watching him. He refused her help in getting up to relieve himself; his bowl of stew was left untouched. The cough returned, and Sade listened to his labored breathing with fear instilling in her heart.

By the time the sun rose once more, Sade found herself in the small home of the herbal healer. She stared at the plants that hung from the low ceiling and the walls that were lined with jars of herbs and powders as Anita looked through one of her books. Taking a small bottle from a cabinet, she pressed it into Sade's hands.

"I can give you this," she said, "but I can only say that it will help ease the pain."

"You mean—" She felt an uneasiness shiver through herself, and tried to hide her shaking hands.

Anita nodded at her unsaid words. "I have only seen something like this once before, Sade, but I know the results."

Tears sprang in Sade's eyes at what those words meant. She thanked Anita and gave her two coins for the medicine. She clutched the bottle to her chest and hurried home, pushing away the feeling of helplessness.

Her father grabbed her arm when she returned, watching her with wild eyes. "What did she say?"

Sade looked away. "She said—she said this would help you."

He didn't seem to believe her, but he took the medicine without a word. She sat and watched the flames flickering in the hearth in silence. She couldn't bring herself to look into her father's dull eyes, not with what Anita had told her.

She kept asking herself, *is this real? Is it really happening?*

As the hours turned to days, he grew worse, the coughing making his frail body convulse in shuttering pain. Each time, Sade turned her head away in horror. She rubbed his chest with oils and gave him Anita's tincture, but nothing seemed to help.

She would look up to find him watching her with black eyes, asking for what she had been told, but she would turn away and say nothing.

Chapter 10

It had been three days since he had last walked freely. In that time, he seemed to have fallen into a state of unknowing, where the outside made no difference to him.

She sat down beside him to give him the medicine and massaged his aching bones. When she reached out and drew back his covers, he looked up at her.

"She said I would die, didn't she."

Sade looked away at the frankness of his words.

"You don't have to hide it from me."

She saw, in his gaze, that he already knew, but when she nodded, he closed his eyes. "She could be wrong."

He shook his head, reaching out to her. "My time has come."

To hear those words from his mouth broke the thin walls she had put up to hold herself. She cried, holding his thin hands in hers.

"I'm sorry, Papa."

He clasped her hand. "There is something I must tell you, Sade. Something I should have told you a long time ago."

He looked past her with tired eyes, and for a long moment he said nothing. Sade held her breath. Finally, he sighed and closed his eyes.

"Before I met your mother, I was married to another woman. We had a daughter, her and I—"

Sade gulped, her voice coming out in barely a whisper. "You mean, I have a sister?"

He opened his eyes and nodded.

Sade looked away, at a sudden loss for what to think. She had known that he hadn't lived with her mother long before she had been born, but never, ever, had he even hinted at this previous life. She had always thought that he had been a solo wandering man. Not a husband.

She got up and went to the window. The sun was setting, lending a warm glow to the sky. She stared at the clear serenity of the quiet world, wishing it would clear the swirling confusion that was seething within her.

"Why didn't you tell me?" She asked, not looking away from the glowing sky.

He closed his eyes again, his jaw working. "It was too painful."

Sade spun around. "Why? You are too ashamed of your own past?"

He shook his head, reached out to stave her anger. "You don't understand—"

"Don't understand what? Don't understand why you couldn't bear to tell me something that I have the right to know?" Sade threw up her hands. "You're right! I don't."

"No, please…" He coughed, his wheezing lungs attempting in vain to clear themselves. When the fit passed, he dropped back on the pillow and rested in a moment of exhaustion.

His obvious pain stopped her words; he was so utterly helpless. He beckoned for her to come closer, and she sat down slowly on the edge of the bed.

"Just listen, please." He rested a hand on her leg. "It is a sin among our people to love the Gadze, Sade, but I renounced that for love of your mother."

"Gadze? Papa, what—"

He groped for her eyes. "I am saying that I am a Romani, Sade."

Her jaw dropped. Things started to click in place in her mind, things that happened too fast for her to understand or make sense of. Her head was throbbing; light weight of his hand pressing against her leg felt as heavy as a stone. Suddenly it was much too hot inside, and she got up and rushed out the door.

The cool night air hit her with a blast; welcome against her hot face. She ran, faster than she had ever run before. Her feet barely touched the ground as she flew blindly across the hills. Tears blurred her vision, and her heart thumped wildly in her chest. In the tall grass on the top of her hill, she collapsed to the ground and cried.

Nothing seemed to make sense. Or rather it did, but it was all so different, so upside down from everything she had thought was true. She began to understand, perhaps, why he hadn't wanted the Romani to know who she was, if it was indeed banishment among his people for leaving them. But why had he never told her?

And a *sister*?

Sade rested her head on her knees. Who was she? She tried to imagine her, a Romani woman who was maybe near her age. She would probably be tall, like her father...

Fantasies whirled in her mind. She thought about her reflection on a dark window, and thought that maybe she wasn't too far off from being a Romani. Yet what did that mean to her? Would she suddenly renounce the life that she had always known and run off with a kumpania?

She pressed the palms of her hand into her eyes, tried to clear her mind. The thought of her father lying perspiring in his bed passed before her eyes. Would she really loose him? Where would she be, then?

Dreary, she pulled herself to her feet. She walked home, questions burning in her mind. Overhead, the stars passed slowly across the sky. She remembered when her father used to tell her stories of the constellations: the warrior, the queen, and the bear. That was before he stopped coming to the hill, sometime around when her breasts stared to grow and her cycles began.

When she opened the door, he was watching her. She carefully closed it behind her and slipped off her shoes, all the while feeling his heavy gaze on her back. Taking a deep breath, she pulled up a chair beside his bed, took his hand, and met his gaze.

"I'm sorry, Papa."

He squeezed her hand very lightly, but she could feel the forgiveness in his dying strength. "I should have told you," he said in a hoarse whisper. "You were right; I was ashamed."

She pressed her mouth into a smile, her eyes glistening. She let the moment of silence pass, and then asked, "Who is she?"

"Her name," he wheezed and coughed, "is Kana."

Chapter 11

Sade sat in stunned silence. Whatever sense of peace she had gained on the hill was gone. Her first emotion was a jumping joy, then surprise, anger, and sorrow. Like leaves blowing in the wind the feelings swirled around her. She closed her eyes in the gale, the grip of her father's hand the only thing keeping her from being swept away.

Even then, she felt that strength slipping, his hand falling from hers. Suddenly her eyes blew wide open, and she cried out.

He stared at her with eyes no longer seeing, his frail hand limp in her grasp. She uttered a scream, yet she didn't know if the sound passed her lips or not. Tears fell in earnest; she laid her head upon his still chest.

She didn't know when she stumbled away into her own bed, nor how much of the day had passed before she pulled herself up again.

And then, she didn't know if it was real or a dream.

Chapter 12

The townsfolk buried Jo Whitman at high noon, their hands laying pacifying gestures on Sade's shoulders as they passed. No one could penetrate the transparent walls that enveloped her. Anita took her home and gave her tea, but she felt uncomfortable with the strange woman and by nightfall she was stumbling home alone.

She drifted in and out of consciousness, her mind attempting to make sense of what had happened to her. Darkness settled in the lowest part of her heart, and anxiety cradled itself in her stomach.

In the dusky forest she walked through, she could see light glimmering far off her path, just hidden by brambles and thorns. Sometimes she would stop and look at it, remembering feelings of happiness, but the thought of traveling through the hardship to get there made her turn once again down the dim path. Deeper and deeper she went, the light moving farther away behind her.

She came to a gateway, and she looked back over her shoulder, somehow knowing that if she crossed the threshold she could never come back again. Ghosts of her memories beckoned to her from the shadows. The images of her laughing childish self, the twinkle in the eyes of her father. Nemea and Kana were there too, shimmering just out of reach.

She looked into the eyes of her sister, who stood watching her. Sade took a step towards her, reached out her hand. But it closed on nothingness, the silvery form shifting forward, eluding her. Kana began walking back the way she had come, her silver skirts barely bending the blades of grass, and without hesitation, Sade followed.

Chapter 13

She awoke with a start, the vision of Kana fading from her mind. She lay under her covers, sunshine spilling through the windows, filling the room with bight warm light. She took a deep breath, stretching her arms above her head.

Her feet padded across the floor to the door, and she looked out. The world seemed to sparkle in gold. A butterfly flitted across her path, landing on a white flower and drinking the sweet nectar. The sun was warm on her cheeks; she closed her eyes and lifted her face to the light.

The emptiness was still in her heart, yes, but instead of pain she enveloped it with light, nurturing the wounds. Her mind was clear; calm.

She knew, in that moment, that she had to move on, and leave this time and place behind her. Without rush she gathered her things; clothing, food, flint, her father's knife. She held it in her hand, the handle worn smooth from the countless times he had used it, and saw her reflection in the blade.

I am smiling, she thought.

When night fell, she sat before a small fire, toying with her father's favorite hat. She took the worn partridge feather from the brim and tucked it into her dress. Then she gave it to the fire. The flames leapt along its brim, slowly turning it to memories and ash. When the fire burned low again she fell into her bed for one last time, falling asleep with a smile on her face.

She picked the road westward, remembering faintly that Kana had spoken of the Bromberg Fair being in that direction. She reasoned, though, that even if she was wrong that it did not matter; she was a free soul with the world to travel.

Her pack bumped comfortingly on her back as she walked. Freeness infiltrated her being. She sang with the birds and spread her arms wide in the breeze. The road she traveled was narrow but worn, and in some places deep ruts cut into its surface. It curved through trees and meadows; over a river flowing down from distant mountains.

She passed a farmer teaching his son how to herd their flock of sheep, and the older man tipped his hat in her direction. Another horse and rider passed her at one point, but otherwise the road was empty besides squirrels and an occasional hare.

She didn't know where, exactly, the road would lead her. She knew only her goal, her ending point, was the Bromberg Fair.

The first night, she slept under the protection of towering oak trees that grew alongside a farmer's field. She could hear cows mooing in the distance as she ate her simple meal of bread and cold meat. Then she lay in the soft grass, pulled her blanket around her, and watched the stars come out between the shifting leaves.

The next morning she went to the farmer's cottage to ask for fresh water. The woman who opened the door had a jolly smile, and she welcomed Sade inside. Three young children looked up from the floor where they played with blocks and little carved men, but they soon disregarded her and went back to their game.

"You're traveling alone?" The woman asked in an Irish lilt, handing her a pitcher brimming with cold water.

Sade tipped it to her lips and nodded.

The woman raised her eyebrows. "You're brave. I hear the Gypsies are about this time of year."

"I am not afraid."

The woman shrugged her wide shoulders.

"Jamie," she said to one of her young ones. "Go and get this nice woman some cheese from the cellar."

"No, no," Sade protested as the boy stood up. "You needn't do that for me."

"Acht, 'tis nothing." She waved it away with a plump freckled hand.

The boy returned, holding out a lump of cheese wrapped in white muslin.

"Thank you, Jamie," Sade said as he thrust it into her hands.

"You are heading west, then?" The woman inquired, turning a huge ball of dough onto her floured table.

Sade nodded. "Yes. To the Bromberg Fair."

The woman grinned. "Aye, I remember going there once. 'Twas a crazy place. Young lass like you will like it though; plenty of handsome young men." She winked.

Sade blushed, turning away in context of putting the gifted cheese in her pack. The woman chattered on, pounding the dough with strong arms.

"My husband can take you a few miles down the road, if you'd like," she said. "He is leaving to deliver milk after we eat."

"That is too kind of you," Sade protested again.

"Acht, don't worry." She gestured for Sade to take a seat. "It isn't often that I have company. I am Fray, by the way."

Sade offered to help, and ended up standing beside Fray and forming loaves as the woman chattered on. There was no way she could get a word in edgewise, and she worked with an amused smile on her face.

When Fray's husband came in, they sat down to a hearty meal of potatoes and stewed beef. The three children laughed and played with each other even at the table, and there was no shortage of happiness among the family.

After they had eaten, Sade bade Fray goodbye. The jolly woman stood at the door and waved as the farmer's cart disappeared around the curve. They sat mostly in silence, the only sound the sloshing of milk in its canisters, the clip clop of horse hooves, and the creak of old wheels.

After a while, the farmer pulled to a halt where the road split in two, and gestured to the one on the left. "That is the road to Bromberg," he said.

"How long, do you think it will take?"

He looked down the road, as if calculating it by how far he could see. He shrugged. "Maybe a week or so, on a good horse and earnest travel. I don't know how long it will take on foot."

"Well, thank you for your kindness," Sade said, climbing down over the wheel well.

He tipped his hat. "My pleasure. If you are ever here again, please visit. It did Fray good; she gets lonely sometimes."

Sade grinned with a nod, stepping back as he whistled to his team. He waved to her as they lurched forward. Sade watched him go, then turned down the other road, shaking her head with a smile on her face.

Three days, she walked, in good weather and fair spirits. She passed multiple homesteads, asking for water at some, and passing by the others. No one was quiet as outgoing as Fray had been, but then she wasn't really sure if she wanted them to be.

In one small village, she bought new shoes with some of the few coins she had saved from laundering, but she didn't tarry long. Something was rolling inside her, and she didn't want to stray too far from her path.

Every day she thought of Kana; what she might say to her when they first met again. She imagined the look on her face, the surprise when Sade told her who she was. Kana would laugh, she thought, and hug her, welcoming her into her life.

There were times, though, when she would suddenly see herself from an outsider's perspective, and wonder if she really had gone crazy. Who suddenly got up and left their life on a dying man's word, much less to follow a Gypsy?

She would falter, then, and look down the road she had come.

Maybe I should go back, she told herself, as the days counted upon themselves. *Maybe I should go and do honest work* —

The thought of growing old with her hands plunged in dirty washing water urged her on.

At least, she hoped, Romani life would be better than that.

Chapter 14

Morning dawned, one day, to find her curled up beneath a low bowing pine. She looked up at the gray skies, where clouds threatened to let loose their anguish, and felt the first glimpse of fear since she had set out on her journey.

Cold fingers tore apart the last of the cheese from Fray, and she munched on a crisp apple from a tree she had found heavy with fruit. She wrapped her arms around herself in the cool air as she ate, suddenly remembering the warmth of her father's fire.

What have I done? She asked herself.

Her face clouded in mirror image of the sky above as she suddenly felt empty and alone. There was still no difference in the swirling skies, and drearily she pulled herself to her feet and coaxed herself to keep going. She had gone not more than half a kilometer when the first fat raindrops splattered on the road around her. It turned quickly from a light drizzle to pouring rain, and Sade found herself running through splashing mud to whatever shelter the trees could give her.

Huddled beneath a bush, she was soaked cold to the bone within moments. The rain plastered her hair to her face, and her clothing clung to her body. Shivering cold, she pulled her knees to her chest and looked out at the nonstop drift of water and the distant roll of thunder.

There was no telling the rain on her face apart from tears. She didn't cry of sorrow; rather it was of loneliness and loss. The happiness she had held for so long slipped away with the sun, leaving behind only weary darkness.

The sky grew dark; lightning flashed. She curled up into herself, her body pressed against the muddied ground, wishing for home. The pine needles pressed lines into her skin and clung to her hair.

They found her, hours later, drenched and frozen in the downpour. She looked up at the familiar sound of hoof beats, muffled this time by the sopping ground. Her eyes grew wide when she saw a kumpania; her heart leapt.

She reached out, fearing that they wouldn't see her, and yet too exhausted to wave them down if they didn't. The Romani didn't miss the bright bundle out of place in the storm.

There was a shout, and a man jumped down from his vardo. He ran to her, rain streaming through his dust-colored hair.

"You shouldn't be out here in this," he cried, strong hands reaching out to help her up.

Sade stared at his gray eyes in numb shock. Her shivering body fell against his as he helped her stumble up the muddy slope to the road.

She blinked, cold and confused, as the back door to the vardo swung open. He lifted her inside, into the hands of a young Gypsy woman. The door closed again, engulfing them in musty dim light, and a moment later the vardo lurched forward.

Sade blinked, her eyes adjusting to the light.

The young woman was kneeling beside her. She began peeling off the layers of her drenched clothing, stilling Sade's protest.

"What were you doing outside on such a wild day?" She asked, wrapping her in warm blankets and setting aside her sopping clothes.

Sade felt her jaw start to chatter, and she stumbled over her words. "I—I am traveling," she whispered.

"Ah." The woman sat back on her heels, looking Sade.

She didn't look much older than Sade, though the lines on her face suggested that she had already grown fully into being an adult. Her skirt was bright red, and she wore an orange brocade coat.

"Where are you going?" She asked.

"Bromberg."

A smile grew on the young woman's face.

"Us, too," she said. She cocked her head. "Why would a Gadze like you travel so far to go to a Romani fair?"

Sade closed her eyes for a moment, sinking into the warmth of the blankets.

"Gadze?" She asked, faintly remembering the foreign word her father had said.

The woman shifted her gaze away. "You aren't a Romani, are you?"

Sade bowed her head. "I don't know, anymore," she whispered.

The woman raised an eyebrow, shaking her head slowly.

"My name is Esmae," she said, settling down on a pile of pillows and blankets.

"I'm Sade."

Esmae nodded; pulled a thin book into her lap. Sade watched as she read, her eyes barely moving across the page, the vardo rocking them as gently as a mother rocking her child do sleep. The dim light made her eyelids grow heavy as she slipped farther into the welcoming warmth.

Chapter 15

She awoke with a start to jumbled commotion. Blinking, she opened her eyes to the cold, bright light pouring through the door. Esmae's dark head appeared as she walked into the vardo, carrying a basket of wild greens.

"You are awake!" She said, setting the basket down and kneeling before Sade.

"Where are we?" Sade sat up and rubbed her eyes.

"We've stopped for the night. Are you hungry? Rajsa and I made some stew."

Sade reached for her shirt, which was folded neatly beside where she slept. "Who is Rajsa?"

"My brother; the man who found you." Esmae stepped over her. "Come out when you're ready," she said, closing the door behind her.

Left alone, Sade looked around the vardo as she pulled on the dry skirt Esmae had laid out for her. Beside her, there was a small iron stove, and beyond that there was a wide bed built up behind a sheer curtain. There were lanterns built into the walls, the wax dripping down from the unlit candles, and a mandolin case half hidden under bright pillows and a woolen blanket.

Sade stepped down the vardo steps and into the bright green light that always came after a storm. Everything was wet, and the air was heavy with moisture. They were stopped along the edge of a vast field, the beginnings of a forest rising up behind them.

She blinked in the bright light, looking around at the numerous vardos that were halted in a rough semi-circle. Dotted among them were cooking fires surrounded with people, and beyond them the horses grazing happily on the lush grass. It was so much bigger than Kana's kumpania, and suddenly Sade was wishing for the single fire.

Esmae crouched beside her own small fire, stirring a bubbling concoction. Across from her, Sade vaguely recognized the man who had found her. He looked up as she approached, his slate eyes darting away when they met hers. A white scar ran down his cheek, stretching taut as his jaw tightened. Sade thought, as she knelt down beside Esmae, that he looked sad; sadder than he should be on such a beautiful day.

"Here," Esmae said, ladling some of the steaming stew into a wooden bowl and handing it to her.

Sade cupped the bowl in her hands, looking around.

"There are so many of them," she whispered in awe as she looked from one vardo to the next.

Esmae followed her gaze, then nodded. "Not many kumpanias are this big," she agreed.

"Dada!"

A young girl ran up to them, her curly black hair falling in childish ringlets to her shoulders. Her creamy brown sweater hung past her knees, and out from under it poked two leather-clad feet. She halted when she saw Sade, the childish joy suddenly hiding behind guarded wariness.

"It's alright, Jonah," Rajsa said, reaching out a hand to the uncertain girl.

Cautiously, she approached, and Rajsa scooped her up with a tenderness that Sade didn't think was capable for such a hard looking man. He whispered something in her ear, and the girl smiled, thought her eyes never left Sade's face.

"Here, Jonah," Esmae said softly, handing the girl a small bowl.

The little newcomer watched Sade as intently as Sade watched her. Rajsa absently fondled her ringlets as they ate.

"You are going to Bromberg Fair?" He asked after a while.

Sade looked up, startled, and nodded. "Yes," she said, draining the last remains of stew from her bowl.

"Do you want to travel with us there?"

Both Esmae and Sade looked up at the same time, surprise etched across their faces. Rajsa had spoken to Sade, but his eyes were on Esmae. Sade saw her open her mouth in protest, but something in his eyes made her stop. Slowly, she set down her bowl.

"Jamal would never allow that," she said, glancing at Sade from the corner of her eye.

Rajsa let out a heavy sigh, and laid a kiss on the top of Jonah's head. "Jamal needs to learn that not all Gadze are bad."

His steely eyes never left Esmae's face, and Sade looked between the two of them in confusion. Esmae watched him for a moment longer, calculating something in her mind. Then she turned to Sade.

"Do you *want* to come with us?"

Sade took a deep breath. She felt surprised at the offer, but at the same time it felt like a puzzle piece falling into place. The storm, Rajsa, the offer. She looked at the man, trying to understand what he was thinking. There was a small part of her that was afraid of the dark stillness that seemed to hang over him like a cloud, but she felt no danger. And Esmae was welcoming enough.

"I — I guess," she said hesitantly.

He nodded; Esmae smiled. She reached out and laid a hand on Sade's leg.

"I am glad," she said.

The tension that had been held taught in the air fell slack, and Sade stood up to help Esmae wash their dishes.

"Who is Jamal?" She asked, dipping the bowls into a bucket of cold water.

Esmae snorted, taking the clean dishes and stowing them inside the vardo. "He is to our leader, to some extent," she said. "Or, at least, that's what he thinks he is."

Sade frowned, still not really sure what she meant, but a dark look had crossed Esmae's face and she didn't ask any further.

Rajsa came and stood at Esmae's shoulder, whispering something in her ear. The Gypsy woman nodded, and looked up at Sade.

"Come," she said, laying aside the worn cloth she had been using to dry the stew pot.

Sade followed them to where a group of men and women were gathered around the steps of an elaborate vardo.

An older man sat on the steps, a map spread across his knees and a pipe drooping from the corner of his mouth. The hum of voices stopped as they approached, and all eyes turned to watch them.

The old man took the pipe from his mouth as Rajsa went up to him. They bent their heads together, and as they spoke his eyes never left Sade's face. There was no mercy in his stare, and she shifted uncomfortably under his gaze.

Finally, he spoke. "You want to come with us to Bromberg?"

Sade nodded. "Yes. If you will let me travel with you."

A bitter look crossed the man's face. "Your people have not done us good."

Sade stepped back in surprise. She suddenly felt like she was a naughty child, drawn before the king with no hope of repaying for what she had done.

"I am sorry," she sputtered. "I didn't know."

The man leaned forward, ignoring what she had said. "You expect us to take you to Bromberg?" His eyes flashed. "Who do you think we are?"

Rajsa laid a hand on the man's arm. "That is enough, Jamal," he hissed.

He glared at him. "She is a Gadzo," he said, hostility interlaced through his voice.

"Jamal, she is as good as lost. She travels the same path we do. Is it so in your heart to leave her behind?"

Jamal opened his mouth, but there was something else that shifted behind his eyes, and he didn't speak. His eyes rested on Sade's, and he held her gaze so strongly that she didn't dare look away. There was something in his eyes that was a warning, and when he spoke, his words were directed at her.

"Do not shame us, girl," he said harshly.

He glared at Rajsa as he stood up, throwing the map to the ground. Before he disappeared into his vardo, he looked at Sade again, and that look appeared in his eyes again. Something of softness; there, and then suddenly hidden again behind cold steel.

The slam of the door closing fell on silence, and for a moment no one moved. Then Sade felt a touch on her sleeve, and she followed Esmae back towards the vardo.

"What..." Sade cast a glance over her shoulder, still confused and unsure.

Esmae sighed. "Jamal...he doesn't like the Gadze. I am surprised that he has let you come with us at all."

Sade shook her head, still not understanding. "But who are the Gadze?"

Esmae glanced at her, her eyes quickly flicking away. She muttered something under her breath. "It is what we call the non-Romani," she said finally. "And that is *not* a compliment."

Sade halted. Esmae didn't stop; there was stiffness in her gait.

Gadze.

Sade pressed her fingers to the sides of her head, trying to clear her mind. A dark rock settled in her heart as she realized that she had agreed to travel among a people who hated her, that she was on a journey to find someone who hated her people.

She began to run, run away from the ring of vardos. What had she done, throwing herself among these people?

"Sade!"

She heard muffled footsteps in the grass behind her, and over her shoulder she saw Rajsa standing at the edge of the kumpania. Slowly, she stopped and turned to face him. Her heart was thumping in her chest, from fear and confusion.

"Where are you going?" He stood tall and still, his hands thrust deep in his pockets.

His eyes were on her, and she found herself looking away. She couldn't bring herself to meet his eyes. Not now, when she knew what the Romani thought of her.

"I—I don't know," she said, too bewildered to think straight anymore.

"I told you that you could come with us," he said, stepping forward slowly as if to not scare her away.

Sade gripped her skirts, biting back the unwanted tears that welled in her eyes. She just wanted him to go, to leave her behind—she wanted them all to disappear, so she could go back to her old life.

But my old life is gone, she reminded herself, and she sank to her knees.

"Sade." Rajsa threw a glance behind him, and then closed the last steps between them. "Sade, I'm sorry." His voice was rushed. Afraid, almost. "It will be alright."

She couldn't hold back the sobs, and she crumpled shaking against his chest. He held her awkwardly as her tears wet his shoulder, and looked at a place in the sky far beyond her head.

"I don't know what to do anymore," she cried.

"Shhh," he whispered in her ear. "It's alright. We'll bring you to Bromberg. I promise."

The words fell into the deep despair that she felt within her, but it was something for her to cling onto in the darkness. Slowly, her sobbing stopped, and then she pulled away from him, ashamed and appalled to have cried in his presence.

She looked away as he stood up, lingered a moment, and then left her. When he had gone, she breathed easier, and she pressed her wet eyes with her sleeves. She sat there for a long time, until dusk began to fall.

When she did go back, she silently ate the bowl of food Esmae gave her, and then curled into a ball on her makeshift bed.

She lay there in the darkness, listening to the Romani laugh and talk by the light of the flickering fires. Her despair began to lessen somewhat, and Rajsa's words echoed in her mind.

We'll bring you to Bromberg – I promise.

Chapter 16

They broke camp early the next morning, and were already on the road by the time the sun had fully risen. The Romani spoke of unrest among the Gadze of these parts, and they didn't dare stay longer than they must. The carts wobbled and turned over the bumpy road, singing their own creaking song as they went.

Sade sat beside Esmae on the vardo seat, watching the fields roll by, listening to the birds and the rumble of speech among the Romani. Rajsa had disappeared, and Jonah ran with the children, playing at their own little games as they laughed and sprinted among the wagon wheels.

"Why are you going to Bromberg?" Esmae's soft voice broke through her absent thoughts.

Sade caught her bright eyes. "I am looking for my sister."

Esmae cocked her head in surprise. "Your sister?"

"Yes." Sade shook her head, still surprised at the words that felt so foreign on her tongue.

"Why will your sister be at Bromberg?"

Sade took a deep breath, looking out at the lush pastures that they slowly rolled past.

"My sister," she said slowly, "is a Gypsy."

Esmae rested her chin in her palm, holding the reins in one hand. There was a grin in her voice as she glanced at Sade out of the corner of her eye. "You didn't say that you were a Romani!"

Sade shook her head. "Am I, though?"

Her question was more to the world around her than to Esmae herself, but the woman still cocked her head.

"What do you mean?"

Sade plucked seed heads off her skirt.

"Well," She hesitated. "My father was a, a Romani. He left his band after my sister was born, for my mother." She gulped. "He said, he said that he shamed them when he left for a common woman, and he never told me. Until now."

"What made him tell you?"

Sade bit her lip and closed her eyes.

Don't cry, she told herself. Not now…

She took a deep breath, stilling the shaking in her chest. "He was dying."

Esmae was silent for a moment, and then she reached out and squeezed Sade's hand.

"I'm sorry," she whispered.

As the sun sank lower in the sky, the children ended their games and crawled into their family carts. The woods grew more and more silent, and even the talk between Gypsies ceased.

The horizon had just begun to glow pink when the first sounds of a river met their ears.

"We will stop here," Esmae said. "If the pasture is good, we will most likely stay for a few days so we can work on training the horses."

"You train them to trade, then?" Sade asked.

"Yes – mostly. But we also perform when we can."

"At the Fair?"

Esmae shrugged, guiding her mare to a halt. "The fairs, and whatever town will have us. It is getting harder for us, though. Less people want to hear our music."

She climbed down from the cart and began unhitching the horse. Sade lingered for a moment, tired from the long ride.

She watched as one by one the other Romani brang their vardos to a halt. Men hopped down from their driving seats, stretching their aching limbs and leading the tired horses to the river. As they turned them out in the lush pasture, the women and older children began setting up camp and preparing a meal.

Sade felt lost in the sudden ruckus, until Esmae sat her down, beside the fire she had lit, with a basket of potatoes to peel. Women gathered around, one producing a skinned rabbit and another corn cake. Soon the tantalizing smell of roasting meat filled the air, and there was a pot of thick gravy set in the coals.

As they sat down to eat, they watched Sade, whispering behind their hands. She knew that they were wary of her, but she avoided their pointed gazes.

There was a certain sense of festivity among them, knowing that they wouldn't have to get up at the break of dawn and pack up camp again. After the dishes had been cleared away, the women took up colorful silks and they danced in the firelight to the beat of a drum and the melody of Rajsa's mandolin.

Sade watched them dip and sway, listening to the songs that were laced with laughter. Her eyelids began to droop lower. Esmae stopped dancing long enough to bring her a blanket, her eyes glittering in the light. Sade curled up beside the fire, her face pressed into the sweet smelling grass.

"Sleep well," Esmae whispered. She grinned, and with a swish of her skirts she danced away.

Sade closed her eyes, listening to the mellow song and the calls of the wild night, and finally she drifted off into sleep.

Chapter 17

She fell into a rhythm, with the Gypsies. All day, there was food cooking over the fires, and some of the Romani made trinkets to sell, but life mostly revolved around the horses. It was always the first thing in the morning and the last thing at night to care for them.

Esmae still said that they weren't like other bands who trained horses; that instead they traveled for entertainment. But as Sade watched them with their steeds, she began to doubt that. It became clear to her that the Romani knew that the Gadze were turning away from what they had to offer. It was unspoken that they were shifting towards more horse trade, but no one denied it.

A middle aged man showed up in camp, one day. His face was red next to his scraggly gray hair as he shook his fist angrily at the Romani, shouting about how they contaminated the world. When the women ignored him and went on with their work, he grew furious and called them incompetent brats.

It didn't take the men long to drive him off, taking him by the arms and dragging him away. Rajsa returned with a light bruise beneath one eye. He turned away when Esmae tried to look at it, mumbling that it was nothing.

He didn't look at Sade; his gaze lingered lost on the horizon. The other Romani watched her with pointed stares, though, and she looked away with a thumping heart.

Would they drive her away, too? Because she had a Gadze mother?

Jamal strolled by their fire that night, his face drawn into a scowl. Sade bent her head down when his eyes scrutinized her. She could feel the blood racing in her veins as he kicked at the grass and spit on the ground.

"You *Gadze*," he spat.

Sade's heart beat quickened. She clamped her mouth closed and bent towards the fire, sending up a flurry of sparks as she added another log. Jamal's nostrils flared.

"Did you hear me, girl?" His voice rose. "Gadze aren't nice to the Romani!"

Sade sucked in a deep breath, daring to look up at his ferocious face.

"I am part Gypsy," she dared.

"What did you say?" His voice screeched like a screaming crow. "Speak up, girl!"

She stood up. At his harsh words, she felt the ground slipping away beneath her feet, but she dared not fall down the mountain she had struggled so hard to climb. In her mind, she glanced over her shoulder, and saw far in the distance a dreary life spent alone without ever having found Kana.

"I am part Gypsy," she said, clenching her jaw to keep herself from backing down.

Jamal sneered.

"And I am part God!" He cried.

He leaned closer, his breath strong in her face. He thrust his forefinger in her direction. "Who your parents are mean nothing to me, girl. You have no right to be here, and you know it."

Sade cringed. She felt rocks beginning to tumble away beneath her as an avalanche loosened the slopes of the mountain in her mind.

Jamal spat at her feet and glared, then stomped off into the night. Sade stood there, stunned. She watched as his shadow disappeared, and slowly she turned away from the fire, away from the eyes that watched her.

She ignored Esmae's reaching hand. She stumbled through the dusk to the vardo, letting the door fall shut behind with a bang her. Blinded momentarily in the darkness, she groped for a candle and lit it. Her hands worked methodically as she began to fill her bag with her things that had become strewn about the small space.

The door creaked open, and she froze. She turned, expecting to find Esmae, but it was Rajsa who stood silhouetted in the firelight.

"What are you doing?"

She looked away. "I am leaving."

The words dropped into the silence. His boots fell with soft footfalls, and he stood a hand's breath from her back. She felt a shiver run up her spine as she wondered if he would drive her away.

"You don't have to go." His voice quivered.

"Why do you care?" She said, whirling around and searching in his eyes. "I am nothing but a *Gadze*." She said it like Jamal did, like the word was bitter on her tongue, and felt it like a self-inflicted wound.

"Sade, I—" Rajsa stumbled over his words, and reached out and touched the side of her face.

Sade's heart shook. She felt surprised, confused. There was a look of sorrow in his dark gray eyes, and his touch was feather light. Suddenly she was afraid, more afraid than if he would have come at her with a hard clenched fist.

She pushed past him, the door clashing shut behind her. As she clambered down the steps, she turned away from the fires, her jaw firmly set. Anger fumed in her chest, anger that had no place to go. She suddenly hated the Gypsies, and all their sickening ways.

She heard Esmae call out her name, pleading for her to stop.

"Sade!" She ran through the grass after her. "Sade, wait!"

Sade's footsteps slowed, and then she warily stopped. Esmae came up beside her, grabbing her arm. Her grip wasn't hard, but there was something firm about it that made Sade look up at her.

"You can't just up and leave, Sade!" Esmae cried, without attempting to conceal the bitterness in her voice. "There is a reason why the Romani are still able to keep strong, and that is because we help each other."

"But Jamal—"

"I don't care about what Jamal just said. Even if you are part Gadze, you are also part Gypsy. Rajsa didn't make a promise to you for nothing."

Sade looked away, remembering the unsettling feeling at the memory of that awkward night. She was surprised that Esmae knew of it, but she realized that she and Rajsa must be close. She wondered, briefly, what their true relationship might be, but she pushed the thought away.

"Please, Sade."

"Why? Why do you want me to come with you? Why do you not hate me, like the rest of the Romani?"

Esmae shook her head slowly. She seemed to hesitate. Then, "We made you a promise, Sade. I like you; we all like you, in some way or another." She took Sade's hand. "Give them a chance. They are just wary of you—that is all."

Sade blinked. "What about Jamal?"

"Don't worry. Rajsa will take care of it."

The cloud that had been anger dispersed into a thick fog of confusion, and she let Esmae take her back. She thought, remotely, that this was the second time she had tried to leave, and yet she still had not gone.

Chapter 18

Tension melted in the air. Word had spread through the camp of Jamal's encounter, and Sade felt heavy eyes on her wherever she went. Esmae did her best to be kind, but her words bounced off the impenetrable wall of glumness that had built up around Sade.

She would look up, seeing the children laughing at their games, and find herself wishing she could once more feel happy and carefree like them. She wanted to shake it off, forget Jamal, and laugh with Esmae again, but the darkness clung to her with strong fingers. The effort to let it go was too much.

At noontide, she left behind her work and wandered down to the stream. She sat along the bank, far enough away from the camp to be alone, and let the gurgling sound wash over her. It was peaceful, serene, and for a moment she forgot her emotions.

Undoing the laces of her skirt, she ripped off her clothing, shivering for a moment in the bare air. A moment later, she dove into the swirling waters, sinking in until just her face showed above the surface.

The water was cold as it rushed past her skin, and she closed her eyes, imagining it taking away her dark thoughts. Under the water, her ears could detect only a low rumble of the current tumbling stones along the stream bed. She held her breath, submerged under the surface, falling down, down, down.

With a gasp, she broke into the air, her skin prickling in the light breeze. Her hair plastered to her body, she waded to the shore. She shivered, cold, but felt a cleansing peace. Her hair sent out a spray of fine droplets of water as she rung it out, and then coiled it up once more.

As she dressed, she felt surprise at the fine trickle of blood running down her leg. Looking to the sky, where the faint sliver of the moon had shown last night, she kicked herself for being so oblivious to the tides. She ripped the bottom hem of her underskirt, wrapping the strip around a lump of the thick moss growing at the bases of the trees.

She recalled the fear that had instilled in her heart the first time her blood came. She had thought she was dying, that something terribly bad had happened to her. She hid from her father, away in the woods, tears streaking her face. Eventually, the bleeding had stopped, and she buried her undergarments under a tree.

She never told her father; she thought she was healed. But at the next new moon, the tides pulled at her womb once more. Shaking in fear, she had gone to Nemea.

She had run to her door, barefooted and with tangled hair, pleading for help. Nemea had taken her face in her frail hands, blue eyes sparkling as she whispered the secrets of womanhood. She gave her lumps of cotton and moss; told her not to be afraid. She showed her how to bury the used moss in the ground as a gift to nature.

There was a dull pang in her heart at the thought of Nemea, yet it had grown small compared to the hurt of her father's death. She pulled up her knees and rested her chin on them, welcoming the moment of silence.

She found herself wishing that she could stay there forever, never have to leave and go back among angry people. How she hated Jamal, and his own open hate towards her. She wished she could leave forever, but remembered once more Rajsa's promise to bring her to Kana.

Kana, her sister.

The thought buoyed her spirits, and when she walked back into the camp, she held her head high and greeted the Romani with a small smile. For a moment, her stomach churned when she saw Jamal standing in the shade of his vardo, but she firmly told herself to look away.

I will have nothing do with him, she bade herself.

"Do you need help, Esmae?"

She was working grease into the driving harness. As Sade crouched down beside her, Esmae smiled when she saw her fresh face.

"The river takes away many peoples troubles," she said, handing Sade a piece of cloth and the bridle.

Sade nodded in quiet agreement, settling herself down beside her as she began rubbing the thick yellow oil into the dry leather. It began to shine under her fingers as she worked, and she felt a deep-set content in the manual work.

"Why does Jamal hate the Gadze so much?" She ventured after a while, pausing in her work and looking up at Esmae.

Esmae sat back, the harness resting in her lap. "When he was a boy, they killed his parents," she said. "Ever since then, he has always hated them; viewed them all as one bad person. Even as a young man, he would go out seeking quarrels with the Gadze. He has broken more than one finger in fighting brawls."

"Do all Gypsies view the Gadze like that?"

Esmae shrugged, bending back to her work.

"Yes, and no." She seemed to hesitate. "The Gadze are always trying to force us into a different mold than we want to be. They don't understand that it is our choice to travel, and that we don't want to settle down." She laid a hand on Sade's arm. Her words were hasty. "I mean nothing against your mother."

Sade choked and looked away. "It is fine," she whispered. "I never knew her."

She grew silent, vigorously focusing on the work before her. Rajsa appeared. There was no smile in his eyes, and he grabbed Esmae's arm.

"Have you seen Jonah?" He asked, a trace of fear laced in his voice.

"No." A look of worry crossed her face. "What is it? What's wrong?"

He bent his head, squeezed closed his eyes. Esmae reached out and touched his shoulder, her look pleading for him to speak.

"She hasn't been seen since yesterday, Ez. The Gadze man—"

The thought was left unfinished on his tongue, but already Esmae had sprung to her feet, the harness falling forgotten to the ground. Sade stood up slowly, watching in amazed confusion as Esmae called out and the Romani surrounded around them, listening as she laid out a search. Then they disappeared, some going on foot and others swinging up onto their mounts' backs.

Sade looked in lost despair at Esmae, who waved her away. "Look for her, anywhere you think she might be."

Everyone was suddenly gone, and the only people left were the elders and young children. She noted, with a pang of contempt, that Jamal had stayed too, scowling on the steps of his vardo.

Momentarily at loss of which way to go, she found herself going along the riverbank, past where she had swum. Birds sang among the trees, and she noticed the very beginnings of autumn gold showing on the tips of one of the trees. A squirrel chattered at her from his perch, and then scampered away among the brush.

"Jonah?" Her tentative voice fell hollowly in the empty air, and she hurried on.

In the distance, the muffled shouts of the other Romani drifted away and eventually disappeared altogether. The stream became wider, growing to be a torrent of frothy white rapids rushing over protruding rocks. She pulled herself up the steep bank to the road when it passed under a wooden bridge, standing for a moment and looking in each direction.

The road was wide and well-worn, more used than the ones she had first set off on. A feeling of joy seeped into her at the familiar sense of freedom, and she felt like the whole world seemed to wait at her fingertips, ready to be explored.

Yet as she walked farther along under the draping branches, calling out to Jonah, her heart began to sink. She thought once that she heard a whimpering cry, and she had stopped and spun around, calling out again and again with hope in her voice. Only silence met her hears, though, and her heart quickened as she stood there waiting. Yet for too long the quiet stretched on, and once again she went on.

Suddenly she realized that the sun was dipping low on the horizon. She didn't know how far she had gone, nor how long it had taken her to get there. A shiver ran down her spine, and abruptly she turned and began to run back down the road.

Her heart pounded.

What if they couldn't find Jonah? Then the little girl would have to stay out in the dark all night. Or what if the Gadze really had something to do with it?

She kept shouting, her voice growing hoarse, until finally she went on in silence.

Maybe they had already found her, and would all look up and laugh when they saw her stumble into camp long after darkness had fallen. They would smirk, perhaps, and call her a pointless Gadze.

There was a sharp cry, loud enough to stop Sade in her tracks. She spun around, looking deeper into the growing dusk.

"Jonah?" She called out softly.

There was a moment of silence, and then it came again, the sound of quiet sobbing. Sade ran off the road, diving among the towering thick trees. Branches and dead leaves crackled underfoot, and twigs grabbing at her hair and clothes.

"Jonah…"

There was a shift in the shadows, a flitting movement beyond where she stood. A slender arm and then a tear stained face appeared, and Sade's heart stopped as she rushed to the child.

"Oh, Jonah," she cried softly.

The girl gasped, her grubby hands clinging to the back of Sade's shirt. She burst into tears, soaking the cloth at Sade's shoulder.

"Shhh, it's alright," Sade whispered, carrying her back to the road. "It's okay now; I am taking you home."

As she consoled the girl, she began to quiet, but her grip around Sade's body was still strong.

"What happened, Jonah?"

"A man chased me," she whispered. "I got lost."

"Are you alright, though?" Sade asked, smoothing the hair away from her dirty face.

Jonah nodded, her big black eyes staring into Sade's. She rested her head on Sade's shoulder as she walked. Sade's eyes stung from trying to see in the darkening dusk. By the time she crossed the stream, the weight of Jonah in her arms made them ach, but there was a feeling of triumph in her chest. She had been the one, the only one, to find Jonah.

Sade felt the girl quicken in her arms as they neared the kumpania, and the dancing fires could be seen at last through the trees. The Romani where gathered around one blazing fire, and they looked up as she neared.

Jonah cried out, scrambling from Sade's arms as Rajsa leapt to his feet and rushed towards them.

"Jonah!"

He lifted the girl into his arms and spun her around, burying his face in her locks of curls. The Romani crowded close, and there was laughter and tears as everyone reached for Jonah. Esmae was there, too, and she enveloped Sade in her arms.

"Thank you," she whispered in her ear.

Sade pushed away the words, feeling a rising pride as the Romani smiled at her in turn, nodding respectfully in her direction as they departed. She felt, somehow, that she had restored her reputation among them.

Maybe, she thought, *I will not be shunned by them after all.*

She was about to turn away and go back to Esmae's fire when Rajsa stopped her, Jonah still clinging to his hand.

"I can't begin to thank you for what you have done, Sade," he said hoarsely, looking her in the eye for the first time since she had come.

Suddenly shy, she looked at the ground, toeing the grass with her boot. "It was nothing," she whispered.

"You saved her life."

"I—" She met his gaze, the words stopping in her throat.

She felt so confused by this man. It seemed that at one moment he was cold and bitter, the next soft and kind. She shook her head. "I only did what was right."

She left him there, and wandered back to the fire. Esmae spooned stew and a hotcake into a bowl for her, then settled back to watch the fire.

Sade ate like a ravenous wolf, the steaming goodness disappearing quickly from her bowl. After she had licked the last crumbs of hotcake from her fingers, she set aside her bowl and leaned back on her elbows beside Esmae.

"Who is Jonah, really?" She asked.

Esmae tucked a stray strand of hair behind her ear, stared off into the darkness.

"Rajsa married a woman when he was young," she said, "like the Gypsies often do. Her name was Jonah. They were sweethearts from the beginning; he did everything for her. Five years ago, Jonah got pregnant. They were so happy, Sade. Rajsa seemed to talk nonstop of raising a family, and he even began work on his own vardo." Esmae took a deep breath. "Childbirth was not easy for Jonah, and after laboring for two days she died."

Sade gulped, looking away from the Gypsy woman. She had guessed something like that, maybe, but to hear it in stark words cut a dagger into her heart. So she and Jonah had something in common, then, to never know their mothers. She saw Esmae's eyes glistening in the firelight.

"They saved the babe, and Rajsa named her after her mother. It broke him, Sade, when she died. If the infant hadn't been saved, I can't bear to think what would have happened to him. Even as it is, he can barely hold on sometimes."

Esmae fell silent, brooding in her own thoughts. Sade stoked the fire, her mind turning. She felt a sudden sympathy towards Rajsa, her heart aching for him in a way she had never felt before. The thought of death brought forth strong memories of her father, and she looked away to hide the tears welling in her eyes.

"I am going to sleep," she whispered, resting a hand on Esmae's arm.

The woman looked up and nodded absently, a blade of grass dangling from her mouth. Sade saw her, for a moment, not as Esmae but as Kana, the first time that they spoke under the moonlight. The image disappeared again when Esmae smiled, and Sade turned away.

Chapter 19

The next night, there was music again beside the fire. Something in Jonah being lost had livened a sense of joy among the Romani, and besides, Esmae said it was time for them to practice. Bromberg Fair was drawing nearer and nearer every day, and once more there was talk of moving on.

Sade sat in the shadows, as she so often did, and watched as they danced. Rajsa played his mandolin, and beside him his close friend Vento played a fiddle while another played the drum. Esmae spun around with the other women, and over and over they practiced the steps to their dance. Laughter spilled out into the night, infecting her with smiles.

She looked up when Rajsa set aside his instrument; found herself looking into his eyes. He came up beside her, crouching next to where she sat, and she looked away.

His breathing quickened.

"Sade."

She heard his voice quiver, and she looked up. The skin was stretched taught along his scar, and she remembered what had happened to his wife. She opened her mouth, to tell him that she knew, that she was sorry, but before she could speak he reached out and took her hand.

"Will you dance with me, Sade?"

Her mouth dropped in stunned surprise. She blinked, her heart thumping wildly in her chest.

What was he saying? She saw hope glinting in his eyes, and suddenly she was afraid, confused, and she pulled her hand away.

"I—"

She pulled herself to her feet and spun on her heel, leaving him sitting there as stunned as she was. Her body was shaking and she hugged her arms across her body as she walked away.

Standing in the shadows on the grassy knoll not far from the fire, she looked back. She saw him still crouched, his head hanging in defeat. What had he meant? A shiver ran down her spine as she wondered if he had been hinting that he liked her more than she thought.

She watched Esmae touch his shoulder and start towards her, and she stood still, waiting for her to approach. She needed to talk to her, to know what was going on. As Esmae drew near, though, Sade saw not tenderness in her face as she had expected, but instead bitterness and anger.

"Why did you do that, Sade?" Esmae demanded, flinging a finger in Rajsa's direction. Her eyes flashed, and Sade drew back from the suddenly fierce woman.

"I don't—" She shook her head, her body shaking in confusion.

"Rajsa is a broken man, Sade, and he is barely hanging on. He loves you, can't you see that? Why do you have to walk away from that?"

"Esmae, I didn't know—" Sade stuttered in despair.

"Maybe Jamal is right, and we never should have let you come with us, *Gadze*," Esmae hissed, pointing an accusing finger in Sade's direction.

Tears stung Sade's eyes at her words, and she felt the insult stab deep into her heart. From Jamal, it was one thing, but she had come to love Esmae, and to hear her say that bit deeper than before.

Sade turned away. "I don't know what is happening anymore," she muttered, weeping.

"Rajsa has a shattered heart," Esmae said bitterly, "and you gave something back to him. Damn you if you walk away from that."

"Esmae—" Sade cried out in protest, but the Gypsy had already gone. A new wave of sadness and anger washing over her as she watched her go, but it did nothing against the twisting confusion that battled in her heart. She wrapped her coat closer around her and walked away, her head bent and tears stinging her cheeks.

When the firelight was no more than a pinprick behind her, she collapsed onto the ground and sobbed, curling around herself in the cold. She wanted to slip away and hide, to never go back to the world where everyone she loved was gone and the rest only brought her confusion. The stars danced across the sky as she lingered between dreaming and waking, and only once the shadows of morning appeared on the horizon did she finally sleep.

Chapter 20

She woke with a start, her body aching and tired, her mind numb to the world. She shook her head, looking up at the clear blue sky. The guilty feeling returned to the pit of her stomach at once, and she rolled onto her side and flung an arm over her face. Still, she knew that there was no hiding from what had happened, what she had done.

After a long moment, she pulled herself to her feet and slipped back towards the kumpania. Her head was bowed in shame when she walked once more among the Romani. She looked up only when she came to Esmae's cooking fire, and saw the crouched woman packing away her things.

"We are leaving," she said shortly, standing up and not meeting Sade's eyes. "A boy came from the Gadze; he warned us that they were coming for us tonight."

The shaky feeling lingered in her chest and stomach. She didn't eat when Esmae offered her food. It felt terrible, wrong, what she had done, but she didn't know how to make it right. She didn't even dare ask where Rajsa had gone, even though he was nowhere to be seen.

It wasn't long after that that the vardos rolled one by one out onto the road once more. Wheels creaked as they dipped in and out of the ruts worn into the hard packed dirt. The children squealed with joy to be on the move again, but among the rest of the Romani there was a cloud of grave seriousness. Sade sat in silence beside Esmae on the driving bench of the caravan, her head resting on the wall behind her, and not a word was spoken between them.

The trees that arched over them were now turning brightly colored, not unlike the garb of the Gypsy women. She wondered at how fast they had changed, from only a month ago being brilliant green.

They passed through a small village, no more than a gathering of thatched cottages, but the people there glared and turned away from the passing kumpania. Sade felt the anger in their gaze, and she looked away from their pointed stares.

To think I used to be one of them, she thought.

The camp they set up that night was a temporary one, in a small meadow not far from the road. Everything was laid out so they could leave at first light; the Romani said they couldn't afford to stay longer in unrest lands than they needed to.

In hard silence Esmae set about lighting a fire. As Sade sat across from her, preparing a lump of meat to put in their porridge, Jonah scrambled onto her lap. Her black eyes looked intensely into Sade's, and in her hand she absently fondled a lock of her hair.

"What did you do to Data?"

Sade blinked in surprise. She shifted the girl to sit more comfortably in her lap. "What do you mean?"

"He hasn't come back," she said earnestly, "since you left him last night."

Silence fell on Sade's tongue. What could she say, to this young girl? The unrest shifted deep in her core, for she hadn't seen Rajsa since the night before either. She cupped the girl's face in her hands.

"I don't know what happened, but I wish I did, Jonah. I wish I did."

Jonah looked at her for a while longer, and then left her to run with the rest of the children. When Sade looked up again, though, she saw her standing and watching her, and she felt a shiver in her spine as she wondered how much the child understood that she didn't. She saw Esmae watching her from across the flickering flames. Her face was glowing in the dusky light, but her eyes were hard.

"What did I do, Esmae?"

The words escaped Sade in a whisper, quiet like the tears that welled in her eyes. It seemed to her as though the whole weight of the world was crashing down onto her shoulders, and now she could not hold it anymore. It stripped her of any existence she had known, and left her wary and shaking.

It was a long moment before Esmae spoke. "You were blind. Rajsa loved you, and you denied it. It broke him." She bent to stoke the glowing tinder. "I don't know where he has gone, or when he will come back. That is all."

Esmae stood, and walked past her. Sade reached out, her hand brushing her skirts, stopping her in her tracks.

"Will you forgive me?"

The woman paused, looking regal as a breeze lifted her stray hair away from her face.

"For my brother," she whispered, and continued walking.

Chapter 21

For days they traveled over the rut-ridden roads. The leaves on the trees whispered with color, telling stories that only they could understand.

They took long detours to avoid the small farming villages that spotted the countryside. When they did cross paths with another traveler, they bowed their heads and said nothing.

"This is outcry," Jamal grumbled, "to go creeping like this about the countryside."

"Remember the Gypsies in the far south," the Romani told him. "The Gadze burned their caravans and drove them out with pitchforks and shovels."

As they rode farther west, though, the caution lessened as other kumpanias converged with them on the widening road. Some of the vardos were polished and glowing, with the women sporting abundant golden jewelry, while in others the vardos where barely more than canvas covered carts drawn by aging horses.

By the nighttime fires, they sometimes stopped beside another kumpania and shared stories and songs under the night sky. Esmae wandered freely among the foreign Romani, but Sade found herself staying near their fire. Jonah became her quiet companion, and they spent many dusky evenings curled up together beside the fire. No one spoke of Rajsa.

Sade would find herself glancing back as they traveled, hoping beyond hope to see him riding up on his gray dappled steed. But no; the road behind them was always empty.

No one knew where he had gone. He had left no word, no inkling of his intentions. As Sade lay awake every night, she wondered where he was, and what she would say when she saw him again. The feeling of guilt never left her. It sat heavy in the pit of her stomach; always there, but slowly growing numb.

In the mornings, they would pack up and travel on once more. Before they left, Sade always walked past the last vardos and stood looking back the way they had come. Sometimes Jonah stood beside her, sometimes not. She knew, each time she went, that she would not find what she was looking for, but it didn't stop her.

"Rajsa will find us when he is ready," Esmae assured her, but Sade didn't miss the worried look in her eye.

After Sade returned one morning, Esmae silently took her by the hand and led her to a rise in the tree strewn field.

"There is the Fair," she told Sade, raising her finger to a point in the distance where there was a cluster of bright dots beside a wide river.

They stood in silence as an autumn breeze plucked at their hair. Sade watched the distant gathering, and then timidly raised her eyes to the Gypsy woman. Their gaze met.

"I know you hope to leave us here, Sade," Esmae said quietly, looking again at the Fair. "I just want you to know that I have grown to like you. I'm sorry you met at odds with my brother, but I wish you well on your journey with your sister."

Sade's eyes grew wet at her words, and she looked away and pressed the tears from her eyes.

"I can't begin to thank you for everything you have done for me," she whispered.

For a moment longer they stood, and then Esmae threw her arms around her. To her surprise, Sade found that her arms were shaking as she returned the embrace. Relief washed over her as one of the walls that Esmae had built up between them came tumbling down.

For the last time, Sade climbed up on the wagon seat beside Esmae. Jonah settled between them. The vardo jolted as Esmae guided her steed onto the road behind the other caravans.

Sade felt her stomach churn as the ground passed away beneath them. She was so close, so close to being with Kana again, without lies to separate them anymore. A sigh escaped her lips, and she closed her eyes. What would she say to her, when she met her?

Jonah jumped down from the vardo and joined the other children racing towards the Fair. The grass was lush and thick on either side of the road, and the horses strained at their halters to nibble at the patches growing along the edge.

At long last, they rounded a hill and came into the wide sloping valley where hundreds of vardos were halted. All around, steeds of every shape and size grazed, and Romani men and women intermingled among them.

So many people, and so much laughter, all in one place. Everywhere she looked, Sade found something new; a new person, a wonderful horse. Everywhere, too, there was a sense of giddiness, and when she looked over she saw that Esmae was grinning.

"I love the Fair," Esmae sighed as she drove their vardo a ways past the rest of the kumpanias and then pulled it to a halt. "The number of Romani who come together—" she trailed off, jumping down from the wagon seat.

Sade helped her unhitch the horse, and she led it down to the river. It dunked its velvet muzzle into the water with a chortle of contentment, and then strained against the lead as Sade let it off to graze among the other horses of their kumpania.

She helped Esmae pull the steps of the vardo in place and set up a shallow tent off the side of it. She worked smoothly, but it didn't quell the quickening of her heart. She found herself glancing over her shoulder at the crowds of people, wondering where Kana would be, and when she might finally see her.

"Go, Sade," Esmae finally told her, laying a hand on her arm. "You are anxious to find her."

Sade protested, but Esmae smiled and pushed her on. Her long borrowed skirts swished in the grass as she walked away, glancing hesitantly behind her. Romani looked up as she passed; some nodded in greeting and others smiled. Gaggles of children brushed past her as they laughed and ran, and others played in the shallow grass beside the river.

She walked slowly, eyes searching through the bands of people for a familiar face. Her heart jumped, once, as she walked past a yellow vardo where a woman bent beside the stairs. In the moment before Sade rushed towards her, though, she looked up, and her heart sank as she realized that it wasn't Kana.

There was no sign of Kana, or Van, or any of the other Gypsies. A bad feeling settled in her stomach as she neared the other side of the gathering. Her feet dragged as she slowly turned around and wandered back along the outskirts of the camp.

Maybe they just aren't here yet, she told herself. *We only just arrived, so it is very well that they will be soon behind us.*

Still, it didn't push away the feeling of dread that hung in her heart.

Jonah and Esmae looked up when she returned to their fire. The sun was slowly setting in the west, and the light shone in their eyes.

Jonah ran up to her, chattering about some game she had played, but Esmae gave her a look full of sympathy and understanding. She handed Sade a bowl of cold rabbit and corncakes, her hand lingering a moment on hers.

"Eat," she said, "and we will go and join the merrymaking."

The food slid down her throat as she struggled with a sudden rush of helplessness. What if Kana never came?

When she finished, she stood and followed Esmae through the groups of laughing Romani. Music lingered on the air, horses whinnied, and the delicious aroma of cooking swirled around them. Esmae led them to a particularly large fire, where Vento was playing his fiddle among five other Gypsy men.

Esmae grinned as she loosened her skirts from her belt. She fell into step with the women dancing at the outskirts of the fire. Someone's voice lifted into the air, spiraling around them in whispering enchantment.

Sade stood in the shadows and watched, not daring to join in. She had come far in joining the Romani in their ways, but she couldn't bring herself to lift her skirts and dance with such carefree grace; not yet. She was afraid; afraid of what they might think of her, afraid of what they might say.

It wasn't long before the music turned slow, and the men began to join in the dance. She watched as Vento lay aside his fiddle and took Esmae in his arms, and a smile grew on her face.

So Esmae is in love, she thought.

She watched them dance, feeling a wave of happiness for her friend. Sade thought she seemed deserving, of love. Following close on the heels of that joy, though, was a pang of loneliness. She turned away before the song was done, leaving the laughter behind her.

It was I who created this, she reminded herself. *I left my home, and I didn't know when a man loved me —*

In the vardo, Jonah turned over in her sleep as Sade crawled into bed beside her. She lay in the darkness and listened to the faint sounds of music. Esmae came in a long while later, her face round and glowing in the light of the candle that she carried.

Sade watched behind hooded eyes as she undressed and carefully undid her hair. The woman lingered for a moment, before a small shard of a mirror. Then she smiled and blew out the flame, crawling in beside Jonah with a sigh. Sade shifted, closed her eyes, and at last fell asleep.

Chapter 22

A clatter and then a scream broke the night. Sade jolted awake, terror sweeping through her body. Through the slits in the vardo there was bright red light, and smoke lay heavy in the air. She stumbled out from the binding covers and flung open the door.

A silent cry escaped her lips. Ashes fell around her, melting her clothes, burning her skin. She coughed, wiped her smarting eyes. Esmae was pushing past her, down the steps. Screams cut through the air, mingling with the terrified whinnies of horses. Not twenty yards away, a vardo stood engulfed in flames, silhouetted figures lurching away from it.

Lights, everywhere. Moving shadows, figures, the cry of a child.

"The harness, Sade!" Esmae cried.

She stumbled down the steps in confusion, then realized what Esmae was saying. She grabbed the pile of straps from the ground as Esmae appeared again, leading her mare. The horse pranced away from them, lashing wildly at its halter. Its eyes were wide and white in fear as they threw the harness over her back, shaking fingers clasping buckles and backing her into place between the wagon tongues.

Seconds later, Esmae let go of the lead, and the horse sprang away, jolting the vardo behind her. Esmae ran beside her, and Sade cried out as Jonah appeared at the back door. The girl was screaming, tears of terror in her eyes as she was thrown from one side to the other in the doorway.

"Stay there, Jonah!" Sade ran after them without a second look behind her at the chaos.

She felt someone grab her sleeve. She spun around, her fist falling heavily against the man's face, and then she was running again, stumbling away.

The smoke blinded her; she couldn't see where she ran. She called out to Esmae, but there was no reply. Everywhere, vardos where ablaze with flames. Horses screamed, eyes white in terror; women fell in clumps, sobbing as their life burned down around them.

Tears clashed down her cheeks, uncontrollable sobs of horror convulsing through her body. She could only think to get away, away from the embers falling on her skin, the burning, the pain.

Someone found her, grabbed her around the waist, pulling her away from the horror. She screamed and flailed, and then heard an unmistakable voice in her ear. She twisted in his arms, and found herself face to face with Rajsa. His black eyes were flashing, and the white of his scar reflected the light.

Her first thought was surprise, but there was no more time to think as his strong arms dragged her away. She stumbled and fell; he pulled her on. Beyond the ring of burning vardos, he pushed her down in the tall grass.

She curled up in a ball, her face pressed against the dirt. Sobs racked her entire body; terror and pain froze her senses. He threw himself down beside her, his arms holding her close in a solid cocoon.

The shouts disappeared as dawn slowly crept into the sky. When the first rays of sun burst from the horizon, there was only the distant crackle and hiss of burning embers. Sade awoke with a start from a fretful doze, and was met with a gray silence and the heavy smell of burnt paint and cloth and wood.

She pulled herself up, saying nothing as she looked out at the destruction before her. Rajsa sat up beside her. For an instant, she grew afraid that he might be angry with her, but he only gazed down the valley with a hard expression on his face.

She knew, without being told, that it had been the Gadze. There were burnt circles in the grass, heavy footprints. Caravans that stood in complete ruin. Charred cloth hung from the spines, and the frames sank towards the ground. Small fires crackled from the floorboards and piles of spent belongings. Many of the horses were gone, probably taken by the Gadze or run away in panic.

She covered her mouth with her sleeve at the retched stench that rose up from the rubble. Rajsa slipped his arm around her shoulders and when she looked at him she saw tears forming in the man's eyes.

"All of that ruin." he muttered to the air.

Sade hesitated, and then turned to him. She felt her heart thump; her throat closed.

"I—I'm sorry, for what I did," she mustered.

He turned to her slowly, his eyes traveling to her face. She expected to see hope there, but saw only gray defeat.

"What does it matter, with all of this?"

He stood up, and began to stumble slowly down towards the devastation. Sade felt tears sting her eyes at his words, but she angrily wiped them away.

The memory of his arm lay heavy on her shoulders as she went after him.

They wandered among the groups of stricken Romani; the mothers who crooned and rocked their children, the men who stood still and stunned among the wreckage. Sade felt her heart rise in her throat at the stench, the sorrow.

Of some of the vardos, there was nothing left, nothing at all, only piles of smoldering remains and a layer of fine white ash that covered everything. It seemed that a few of them had escaped damage, but others looked like they had been stopped in flight, with wheels hacked away and the frames bending haphazardly towards the ground.

What had made them do this, she wondered, *to such innocent people?*

Anger made her clench her fists and bite her tongue, and yet it was like a double edged sword as she felt the guilt that it was her people who had done this.

"You!"

In the broken silence she turned, and saw a Romani woman with snarled gray hair. She held an infant wrapped in her arms, and her jaw was set hard.

"You brought them to us, didn't you," she hissed, throwing a fist in the air.

Sade took a step backwards in surprise at the assault, and felt Rajsa's hand steady her at the small of her back. For a moment, she felt a little comfort in his touch, even if it meant nothing.

"You aren't one of us, even if you try to pretend, Gadze," the woman cried in fury.

She just stared. Rajsa guided her away from the woman and the other Romani who were beginning to look in their direction.

"I had nothing—" she began, but Rajsa grabbed her arm and pulled her away.

"Don't aggravate them," he hissed in her ear.

She pulled away from him, rage rising in her chest. How could they even begin to think that she had brought the Gadze here? She felt heat rising in her cheeks as they glared at her as they passed.

She wanted to cry out, tell them that she loved the Gypsies, cared for them, that her upbringing had nothing to do with any of it. Yet she knew that it would only anger them more to know she was the daughter of a banished Romani, so she held her tongue.

She saw two familiar forms coming down from the fields; one large and one small. She ran towards Esmae and Jonah, her arms outstretched. They collided, a jumble of arms, tears, and thankfulness for being alive.

Sade saw the look of surprise in Esmae's eyes when she first caught sight of Rajsa behind her. Jonah had already pulled away and was running to her father's arms.

"You came back!" Esmae cried out softly.

He came slowly towards them, and enveloped Esmae in a hug.

"I heard that the Gadze were coming. I tried to come and warn you, but I was too late." His voice broke.

"It is no matter, Rajsa. The vardo is safe, and we are not hurt."

There was a moment of silence, when Sade knew that they were all thinking of what had driven him away. She shifted uncomfortably, shame rising in her cheeks. It was Jonah, sweet Jonah, who broke the dead quiet.

"I missed you, Data," she said, taking his face in her pudgy hands and planting a wet kiss on his cheek.

"I missed you too, sweetling." He whispered into her hair and closing his eyes to welling tears.

The child laid her head on his chest, and they all turned and walked back up the hill. Esmae had stopped the vardo in a dip amid a grove of trees, and beside it a few other caravans from their kumpania had also come to a halt.

The other Romani who had not already fled were scattered across the hillsides, too; small groups of men and women and what was left of their belongings. Those who had something to share shared it, and others quietly helped in any way they could.

"I've never seen the Romani come together with such union," Esmae whispered in Sade's ear. "We always seem to be pitted against one another's differences, fighting amongst ourselves, and never facing the true enemy."

"Which is?"

"You already know as well as I that it is the Gadze," she replied.

Sade bent her head. "They think it was I, who brought the Gadze here."

Esmae paused for a moment. "Well, let them think that, then. They are wrong."

Sade sighed, sinking to the ground and burying her head in her hands as Esmae walked away. Her throat closed at the open devastation on the Romani's faces, yet she felt grateful that they did not look upon her with hate as they passed.

It seemed that they were lost, milling around with no sense of direction. Already the day was well passed, and they had done no more than sit and speak of what they might do. It seemed that there was nothing more that she might do, other than wait.

Her heart ached, too, for Rajsa. He seemed as stunned as the rest, his head bent wearily towards the ground. Watching him sit there, she closed her eyes, in that moment admitting to herself that she had grown to like the man. And, it seemed, he had left his passion for her burning in the ashes of the great fires.

Chapter 23

As dusky evening fell, the Romani left the tranquility of their grove and wandered back down to the place that had been a merry festival only the day before. Now, under the dark and cloudy sky, there was no joy in the people's eyes. Instead of love, there was devastation; instead of bliss, there was sorrow.

Vento put his arm around Esmae, and together they stood at the edge of the ashes. Sade saw Jamal turn away from them in anger, but the rest of the Romani paid them no heed. In their minds, there was no need to shun them for love out of wedlock. Not in a time like this.

Sade walked away from them, starkly reminded of what she had walked away from that night. In the time that Rajsa had been gone, she realized that she had come to terms with him, but now it was as if he had built a wall between them.

She wandered on, kicking up clouds of ash and stumbling over broken wheels. Suddenly she was thankful that Kana had not been there to see the vardos burn to the ground. She wondered where she was, what had happened to them. Then her heart stopped. Maybe the Gadze had already found them.

She pushed the thought away, but it lingered at the back of her mind. She saw a woman tending to her small child; perhaps she looked familiar. Had she seen her before? No. But maybe.

She looked over her shoulder, to see who was watching, and then hurried forth. The woman looked up in surprise, hugging her boy to her chest.

"Please," Sade said softly. "I only have a question. Do you know the whereabouts of a woman named Kana?"

The woman's eyes grew wide, but she shook her head. "I know nothing."

Sade lingered a moment, but she left them, and went on to the next man.

"Do you know of Kana?" She asked. "Do you know where she might be?"

They all shook their heads, turned away from her. Some drove her away before she could speak; others said nothing. By the time she had stumbled upon Esmae again, her head was bowed in defeat. Not one of the Romani had known of Kana; none could give her hope.

Rajsa walked just beyond her shoulder as they trudged back up the hill towards what was left of their kumpania, but she barely noticed. What did it matter anymore? What of life was left to give, if it all could be taken away with a swipe of the arm and fire?

Esmae came to her the next morning, found her curled up alone in the grass beside the vardo. She looked old, Sade thought, as she crouched down beside her.

"We are leaving," she said, laying a hand on Sade's shoulder.

"Leaving?"

Esmae nodded. "Where there are some Gadze, there are more. The elders among us have decided that we must scatter to the winds, so they cannot destroy us all."

"Where will we go?" Sade asked, sitting up beside her.

She shrugged. "Wherever the road takes us."

Sade looked around at the dissipating people. They walked away from the ruin behind them in twos and fours, barefoot and on horseback, or with a steed pulling with the remains of a caravan. The band of Gypsies from their kumpania loaded their few belongings into the four remaining vardos.

"Why—why not revenge?" Sade asked, looking around at the people, at the low hanging cloud of defeat.

Esmae shook her head. "We are too few, Sade. Even if we were to somehow overcome the hundreds of men in the villages around here, there will always be more, more wherever we go. It is best to go quietly, lay low, and find a place where we are accepted." As she spoke, tears brimmed in her eyes, but she did not let them fall.

"Come, now. Let us go."

Sade pulled herself up and followed Esmae, wrapping her arms around her body.

So this was how it will end, she thought, *in a great exodus away from the past.*

She helped Esmae pack coals from last night's fire into a pot, and she stowed it away in the back of the vardo. Rajsa was buckling the harness onto their steed, and Jonah spent a quiet moment sitting in the grass beside the great wheel.

They had gathered at the back of Esmae's vardo, speaking of where they might go. The men's faces where grim as they laid out their ideas. As they spoke, an old woman appeared in their midst, a tattered shawl wrapped around her shoulders. The lines on her face were ancient, yet there was still life behind her small grey eyes. They stopped, looking at her in surprise. She scrutinized their faces, her gaze landing finally on Sade.

"You," she said, and Sade stepped back in surprise, suddenly sure that she had come to accuse her of leading the Gadze here.

But the woman showed no anger as she beckoned for Sade to come closer, child. Her voice was cold and raspy as she spoke.

"You were asking after Kana, where you not?"

Sade's heart thumped. "You know her?"

The woman waved her away. "Never mind if I know her. The Gadze took their wheels away; they could not come. You will find her in Norman, on the banks of the Tmer. They are stopped beneath the willows."

Sade's breathing quickened, and she heard the words echo in the back of her mind; *stopped beneath the willows.*

"Thank you," she whispered.

The woman bowed her head. She nodded at the other Romani, and then she was gone. Sade glanced at the Gypsies gathered around her.

She saw Rajsa bow his head, and for the first time she realized that finding Kana would mean losing him, and losing Esmae. But if he didn't care for her anymore, did it matter? She was surprised, then, when he stood and went to Jamal.

"So, we will go to Norman?"

Jamal's mouth puckered. "And why do you suddenly think that we will go there? You'd go at the want of that, that—" He gestured helplessly at Sade.

"One road is as good as another, Jamal. And I promised her."

"Since when does a promise mean anything?" He clenched his fist. "Besides, didn't the woman say that the Gadze had taken their wheels?"

Then Esmae stepped in. "We don't know if any other place would be better."

Jamal glared. "I forbid it," he growled.

"Where would you have us go?" Vento asked, coming up behind Esmae. Jamal's hands fluttered in the air as an act of despair. When he said nothing, Vento went on.

"I say we go where there is at least some purpose. I think we can agree that if there is evident danger, then we will not go on, but otherwise I see no harm in trying."

The muscles in Jamal's jaw tensed and his eyes flared, but suddenly his word was nothing amidst the rest of the Romani. He looked at Sade, and for a moment she thought that there was something else behind his eyes, but then he cursed and spun away into the shadows.

"Thank you, Vento," Sade said, turning to where he stood beside Esmae.

He barely nodded, but Esmae flashed the beginnings of a smile. The first smile she had seen since the fires.

Chapter 24

They traveled east as the leaves on the trees began to whither and fall. From the deep chests of the vardos they pulled heavy blankets and thick coats. There was enough grass to keep the horses fed, but they all knew that with each day the winter months were drawing closer.

There was joy in moving again, a sense of excitement for what lay around the next bend in the road. They rarely saw other Romani, but when they did there was laughter and clapping on the back. It seemed that since surviving what the Gadze had done, there was a sense of invincibility.

They gradually went southward, too, and as the distance greatened between them and Bromberg the people of the hillsides grew friendlier. They didn't push their luck, and never stayed in one place for more than three days, but there was more freeness in their living.

And though Esmae tried to hide it, there was no denying the love that blossomed between her and Vento. Her face seemed more often flushed with joy, and sometimes she would slip away at dusk and not return for hours.

It was forbidden among the Romani to love without being married, and men and women weren't supposed to be alone together, but the older of them turned a blind eye to the love. They seemed to think that sometimes, tradition must be let go of in the face of sorrow.

Sade found herself looking away from their love, too. It brought Rajsa's distance even closer to her heart; made her feel more intensely his silence. She saw him watching them, felt an urge to run to him, but she turned away from it and focused her sights on the road before her, on Kana.

A fortnight later, they came to the outskirts of Norman, a sprawling village on the banks of the Tmer River. Farmers's fields sloped down to the tall buildings and crowded streets. Sade felt her excitement return as she stood with Esmae on a hill overlooking the valley.

"We're here," she said in disbelief. "I hope—"

Esmae touched her arm. "She'll be here. Don't worry."

She pointed to the road heading west from the town along the river. "I think that the woman meant that they'd be there. On the other side of town the bluffs are too steep for a kumpania."

Sade stared at the towering trees, her stomach turning. It was the first time that she really realized that she was going to see Kana.

Esmae slipped an arm around her shoulders. "I'll miss you."

Sade squeezed her. "I will miss you, too."

They stood silently for a moment longer. Then Sade took Esmae's hand, and together they walked back to the kumpania.

From the vardo, Sade gathered her few things into the sack. She stood in the middle of the small space, realizing how much she would miss it, and miss all the times she had spent there.

When she stepped down from the caravan, the Romani she had come to know where gathered around. They smiled, wishing her well, giving her a pat on the back. She felt a sudden overflowing in her heart as she was enveloped in their embrace. She felt a twinge of guilt as at last she turned to Esmae, who stood off with tears in her eyes.

"I will never forget you," Sade whispered.

"We will see each other again." Esmae gave her a strong hug. It lasted for a long moment, but at last she stepped away.

They stood awkwardly before each other, unable to think of something to say. Then Jonah raced up to her, something clutched in her hand.

"Data made something for you," she said, holding out her small hand.

Sade knelt down beside her, smiling at the sweetness in the girl's eyes. She let something fall into Sade's hands; a thread of leather, and on it a small wooden moon. Sade gasped, blinking back the tears that sprang in her eyes.

"Your data made this?"

Jonah nodded, a proud look in her face. Then she frowned. "Will you come back, Sade?"

Sade smiled sadly, wondering when she would see the girl again.

"Yes, Jonah, I will come back."

She stood up, tying the leather thong around her neck. The moon fell comfortably against her chest, lingering just above her breasts. She squeezed Esmae's hands and took a deep breath. In the shadows of the trees, she saw Rajsa standing and watching her. Her hand went to her throat, and she nodded softly. She could not see if he nodded back. He slipped deeper into the shadows, and with a last glance behind her she left the kumpania.

Chapter 25

She began to fill with excitement as she walked on.

Despite the late month, the banks of the river grew lush and green, and the oak trees arched over her head in a tall canopy. The path she followed led her down from the low hills, towards the river. Before long it intercepted a wider road running parallel to the river, and she walked away from Norman, searching.

The first sign of the kumpania was the deep ruts leading off the road and into the trees. Sade stopped, looking at where they disappeared among the trees. A piece of blue shown through the leaves: a vardo.

Her mouth ran dry.

What would she tell Kana, in the first moment she saw her? What if she didn't want to see her? Maybe she was still angry with her father for leaving her, and wouldn't want Sade to be there.

She forced herself to swallow. *I have come this far, she thought. I cannot turn away now.*

Taking a deep breath, she walked down the ruts. The piece of blue grew into a caravan, and beside it there was another, and another, and another. And there, to her left among tall birches, was Kana's vardo.

True to what the Romani woman had said, the wheels were gone, strewn in broken heaps of splintered wood around the clearing. It seemed that new ones were being built, under a makeshift lean-to in the trees, but none had been refastened to the axels.

A middle aged woman sat on the steps of the blue cart, a pipe hanging from her lips. Her white blouse hung open to her breasts, and her curly red locks fell around drapes of a silver necklace.

The woman looked up as she approached, raising an eyebrow. Sade didn't know if she was recognized or not. She remembered the woman, but was at loss for a name.

"What do you want?" The woman asked.

Sade looked around; saw the horses grazing in a bare patch among the trees.

"Is Kana here?" She asked, her heat thumping.

"Ah." The Gypsy took the pipe from her mouth and stood up, the door swinging shut behind her with a soft thump.

In the stillness that followed, Sade wondered at how quiet it was compared to Esmae's kumpania. The few children that she could see were playing quietly. Her gaze swung again to the vardo as the woman reappeared, this time someone looking over her shoulder.

"Sade?"

Sade stood where she was, watching the emotions play across Kana's surprised face. She came down the steps and stood before her; not smiling, and yet not angry, either.

"What has brought you here—"

Her words began strong, but faded away, and Sade realized she must have read her mind. Still, she spoke the words that had been heavy on her mind since she first known them.

"You are my sister."

There was a moment of stunned silence as the words settled in the still space around them. Even if both had known, the words were heavier in the raw air.

Kana swept Sade into a hug.

They squeezed each other tightly; Sade laughed through her arms, tears in her eyes. Relief swept through her, that the moment had finally come.

Kana tugged on the end of her scarf and whispered in her ear. "I am glad you came, Sade."

Sade looked at her feet, still surprised to finally be there; ashamed to think she had come so far on a whim. Yet here she was, with her sister among the people of a Romani kumpania.

Kana took her hand, leading her down to the rushing river. They walked among the trees, willow and birch and pine, until the caravans had disappeared from view. As they stood there, watching the water rush past, Sade felt a rising feeling of amazement and joy rushing into her throat that almost made her want to her lift her skirts and run like a reckless child.

"How have you come to find me? What has brought you here, now?" Kana asked, turning to face her.

Sade's fingers ran along the frayed sleeve hem of the coat she had borrowed from Esmae. She looked at the ground beneath her feet, ground that wasn't all that different from that in the woods of her home.

"Papa—Jo—he died." She saw Kana's face grow dark at his name, but there was dampness in her eyes. "He told me, before he was gone, that he was a Romani. That you were his daughter."

Kana's toes traced circles in the dirt. "May he rest in peace," she whispered.

Their heads were bowed for a moment, and then Kana spoke again.

"But you came here, to find me?" There was a touch of surprise, emotion, in her voice.

Sade let out a quiet laugh. "There was nothing left for me there. I loved you, even before I knew you were my sister. I loved the Romani."

"I wondered if I would ever see you again."

"Sometimes I wondered, too. I had thought to find you at Bromberg."

"You went as far as Bromberg to find me?" Kana lifted her face to the treetops with a quiet laugh. "And I wasn't even there."

Sade could see that her heart was touched, and she ducked her head away. "I am glad you were not," she said quietly. "The Gadze came, and burned the vardos. They drove away the horses; ruined the people."

Kana's mouth dropped. "I thought it was bad when they took our wheels away, but this," she shook her head. "This is madness."

They stood there as the sun dipped lower in the sky, talking. They spoke of things deep in their hearts, of things that were trivial and meant nothing. Sade told her how she had met Esmae, of the long journey from there to Bromberg to Norman.

Still, she spoke nothing of Rajsa, though her hand crept to her throat and the small moon that hung there. She knew Kana saw the gesture, and she pulled her hand away, but her sister said nothing.

"But what of you?" She asked, changing the subject. "Tell me your story."

"When Jo left us for the Gadze woman," she said, "Moma's heart was broken. She couldn't look at me without crying. She said I reminded her of Data. I was only a child."

She took a deep breath, looking up at the trees, her eyes lost in thought. Sade watched her, growing awe and love for this woman, her sister, and yet at the same time frightened by all she didn't know about her.

"Moma left—she took her favorite steed and raced away. My elders said that she would come back, after she found Data, but she never did." Kana bit back tears, and gestured for them to keep walking. "I heard about you. I used to be angry that Data loved a different girl more than me. I couldn't understand." She hesitated, glancing at Sade from the corner of her eye. "I'm not sure I still understand."

Sade laid a hand on her sister's shoulder, bending her head in a quiet voice of sympathy. Before this, she hadn't thought what it would have been like after Jo left them.

No, she reminded herself fiercely. He was *my* father, too. And suddenly she was filled with an intense hatred for what he had done, to both of them.

She heard Kana draw a quivering breath. "There is something else, too, Sade."

She halted at the fear laced in Kana's voice. Kana looked away, biting her lip, plucking at the edge of her sleeves.

"What is it?" She could hear the anticipation in her own voice, but in her stomach she felt dread at Kana's tone. Every second that she didn't speak, it grew deeper, sharper, in its pain.

"He came back to us, when you were just a babe; pleaded for us to take him back." Kana burst into tears, but she went on. "I hated you, all pudgy and smiling, and I hated him, for thinking he could come back after what he'd done. I shunned him. I shunned you. I was the one who banished him, never to return. I told him—I told him to take his devil baby and never come back again."

Sade's heart stopped as Kana broke down before her. She was clutching her face, shaking in sobs. She wanted to reach out and comfort her, yet at the same time she felt love and tenderness there was hate and disgust, too.

"You never wanted to know me."

Kana caught her sleeve to make her stay.

"It's not like that anymore."

But Sade turned away from her. She plunged her face in the running current. The freezing cold numbed her cheeks and made her eyes sting.

"Forgive me," Kana cried out, but she did not turn.

Instead, she waded into the middle of the river and stumbled over the stones downstream. The water rushed through her skirt and grew painful on her legs, but still she walked. She walked until she could feel no more, until the pain in her heart had ceased to nothingness.

The words Kana had spoken echoed in her mind, turning over and over again until eventually there was meaning to them no more. She began to shiver, the cold easing deep into her body. She saw, for a moment, how fragile the thread of life was that kept her living; how in a larger sense everything that had happened between her and Kana really meant nothing. They were together, what was done was done, and there was no changing it.

The only thing I can change, she thought bitterly, *is my own path through this time.*

It took strength, for her to step once more on to the riverbank and not let herself drift away in the current. All else left her mind as she stumbled up the steps to her sister's caravan.

Her fingers wrapped around the handle and pulled it open. Kana looked up, her face pale in the lamplight. Sade stared back, unblinking. The silence stretched until it could have been broken with a pin-drop, and still Kana did not speak. Finally, it became too much.

"I forgive you."

The taught muscles in Kana's face relaxed; she let out a gasp of relief. A moment later, Sade dropped to the ground, hugging her shivering body in her arms, and Kana rushed to help her up, to wrap her in blankets and sat her beside the stove.

Slowly Sade's toes thawed, and with them melted all the harsh feelings she had felt for Kana. Her sister spoke quietly as she boiled tea, saying I missed you, sister, and why did you do this to yourself. I love you, sister. Where have you been?

Chapter 26

Dawn broke the next day, and when Sade opened her eyes she saw Kana bending over the small stove. She spoke in low whispers with Van. Beyond the gauzy curtains behind them, the bed was a pile of rumbled blankets. A half melted candle spilled wax onto the floor; thin cobwebs hung in the far corners.

Kana looked up at her, sensing that she was awake, and she came and knelt beside where she lay.

"You are up, sister," she whispered. She handed Sade a pile of dry clothing, and modestly Van stood up, nodded goodbye, and left.

There was a moment of silence when their eyes met, and a quiet grin grew on their faces.

"There's food outside when you're ready," Kana said, leaving her to dress.

She ate with them beside their small fire, and then Sade took a basket of washing from Kana and went down to the river. She needed a moment to herself, to sooth the thoughts that bounced into her head. As she dipped the clothes into the cold water, she wondered at how far she had come in these last months.

Or, she wondered, feeling the odd sensation of discontent that she had felt so often in being in unfamiliar places, had she come nowhere at all?

She looked over her shoulder, where thin laughter and sounds of the Romani working with their horses drifted to her ears, and wondered why she didn't feel entirely content with being there. It was what she had wanted, since the moment she left her home, was it not?

Kana flashed into her mind, smiling and loving, welcoming her into her life. She knew, even though nothing was spoken between them, that she was to stay with them. So why, then, this gnawing feeling?

She felt guilt in the pit of her stomach, remembering Rajsa for the first time since the day before. Sitting back on her heels, she realized that it wasn't being here that troubled her; it was what she had left behind.

Sade looked up at Kana's soft steps; her sister settled down beside her. She followed Sade's gaze across the river, but saw only the shadows and the reflections on the water.

"Willow cries for lost love," she said quietly, her gaze drifting to the majestic trees whose limbs brushed like elegant fingers across the surface of the stream.

Sade looked up as the words hit home.

"How—" she began.

Kana smiled, and patted her hand.

"It isn't hard to see, Sade," she assured her. "Who is the lucky man?"

Sade looked away again. She wasn't really in love, was she? Yes, she had thought he loved her, but since the night he asked her to dance, it seemed that the feeling had left him. So why was there this lingering ach in her heart?

"Rajsa was the one who found me in the storm," she finally said. "It was he who promised that they would take me to Bromberg to meet you." She took a deep breath, fondled the laces of her shoes. "Esmae told me that Rajsa was a broken man, that his wife had died. She said that he loved me.

"I turned away from it, Kana, and now I am all but gone to him."

Angrily, she wiped away the tears that pooled in her eyes. She knew now that she regretted not accepting his dance. She was ashamed at what had happened, and it came back to haunt her.

Kana reached out and gripped her hand firmly. "Do you love him?"

Sade looked up at the trees, willing herself to be strong.

"I don't know," she whispered. "I thought not, but now that he is gone, I don't know." She couldn't help the sobs that clutched her; she fell into Kana's arms. "I am sorry," she murmured, but Kana only held her closer.

When she quieted, Kana pulled away.

"It will be alright. Let it go." She squeezed Sade's hand again and got up. "I love you."

Sade saw the sadness in her eyes, and as she watched her go she wondered what had caused it.

She did her best, after that, to do as Kana said and put that behind her. There were times when it slipped in and caught her unaware, but she began to turn away from it. Still, as she spent the passing days with Kana, laughing and talking, she couldn't help but notice the deeper silence that had come over her sister.

She was sitting beside the cooking fire, preparing a rabbit Van had trapped for stew. Sade stood in the shadows of the vardo, watching, as she bent and slid the chunks of meat into the pot over the fire. Her lower lip protruded just a little bit, and her face was long.

Sade walked up to her slowly, and knelt across from her. Kana looked up, giving her a smile that didn't reach her eyes.

"Kana, what is it?"

The woman sat back on her heels with a frown. "What is what?"

Sade spread her fingers wide against her skirt, the words stalling on her tongue. "It's just—you've been so quiet, so sad."

For a long moment, Kana said nothing, and Sade began to think that she wasn't going to answer.

Finally, she said, softly, "I'm just afraid, that you'll love him and leave me again."

Sade blinked. "Kana, I never meant that. You are my *sister*, and I've traveled so far to find you."

Kana just gazed at her, silently shaking her head. Then she went back to her work, and Sade left. The words hung heavy in her heart as she wondered if she would really leave Kana at the slim chance of love.

That night, Kana swept her up into their dance before she had time to protest. She felt clumsy and awkward among the Gypsy women, but they just laughed and spun her around.

It was the first time she had danced with Romani, and she found herself smiling. Later, she fell exhausted into the bed they had made her on the vardo floor. As she lay there, she laughed at herself as she found herself wishing that the music had gone on longer.

Chapter 27

The woman who Sade had met the first day walked up the steps to their vardo early one morning. She hugged Kana in greeting, and then turned to Sade, who was washing bowls from their breakfast in a bucket of water.

"There is someone here to see you," she said.

Sade stood up, her blood racing in her veins. She knew who it was, even before the woman told her it was a man with a scar.

She set down the bowls with a clatter, glancing for a moment at Kana. There was a blank look full of unwritten emotion in her eyes, and Sade found herself unable to hold her gaze as she let the door close with a heavy thud behind her.

She caught her breath as she stood on the top step.

Rajsa was standing not far off, his hands thrust deep in his pockets. Their eyes met, and she slowly walked towards him, unable to meet his gaze.

"I came to tell you that we are leaving," he said when she neared.

Sade swallowed. She had known that was what he had come to say, but the words still cut into her heart.

Awkward silence fell between them, and she shifted uneasily from foot to foot. She didn't know what to say; what to do. He clenched his jaw.

"Sade—" he drifted off, shaking his head. "I'm sorry."

Her eyes flickered to his, and she saw that he was staring at the ground. "Sorry for what?"

"For what happened between us." He paused, stared deep into her eyes. There was another moment of silence. Then he said in a low voice, "Maybe we will meet again sometime."

He turned away.

"Goodbye," she whispered, not even sure if he had heard her.

She felt tears welling in her eyes, but made no move to wipe them away as she watched him slowly disappear among the trees, his head bent like a defeated man.

An empty feeling settled in her stomach, and slowly she turned to face Kana's kumpania. The pale thread of light between them glimmered, drawing thinner, and then broke away altogether.

Suddenly, she realized that her heart was being taken away from her. In one moment, she gasped, and in the next she was running after him.

"Wait, Rajsa!" she cried, stumbling over fallen branches.

He stopped; turned to face her. A sob escaped her throat as she fell into his open arms. Sade didn't stop the tears that fell down her cheeks as he folded her close to his strong chest, his body shaking.

As they stood there, she felt everything drop away, and then there was only that moment. It seemed as if a final puzzle piece had fallen into place. She realized that this was what she had been searching for, from the moment she had left home and even before that. She had thought that it was Kana, and yet he had always been there.

"Don't leave again," she said in a barely audible whisper. His arms shook, and when she pulled back she saw tears welling in his eyes.

And then his lips pressed against hers.

She shuttered as a tingle ran down her spine. Leaning in, she closed her eyes. All else melted into nothingness, and it was only the two of them.

Rajsa pulled away, leading her down to the wide river. She slipped her arm around him and rested her head on his chest as the watched the river flowing by, the misty colors reflecting in their eyes. There were no words for them for a long moment; only listening, watching.

Her heart thumped heavily in her chest. The fine fingers of confusion and doubt began to slip into her cloud of warm joy, and she closed her eyes, willing herself just to live in this moment.

"Will you come with us?" He whispered in her ear.

She pulled away and faced him. He stood there, waiting, wondering, caught in the still moment of her gaze. She shuttered to think of losing Kana again, so soon after finding her, but in the same breath she knew where her heart lay.

"Jamal won't like it."

"I don't care."

"I didn't think Romani accepted people out of their kumpania."

"You are Romani, though."

She bit back the tears of love in her eyes, her fingers slipping from his as she walked to stand at the river's edge. In the reflection of the water, she saw her life flashing past. The journey to find herself here, teetering on the brink of perfection. She turned and looked at Rajsa from a distance.

A Romani man.

His gray eyes watched her. Her heart was burning in her chest, begging her to say yes. She knew that her love blinded her perceptions, but at the same time there was her love for Kana, and she wondered how she could leave her.

It had been a long journey to come here. She had changed. What would her father say?

A sigh escaped her. She glanced over her shoulder, to the place where Kana's caravan was hidden behind the trees. She was stranded on a tightrope over a deep gap, swaying in the force of her emotions, unable to make the choice of which side to go to. Her footing faltered, and suddenly she was afraid that she would fall to the rocky depths below.

Her footsteps steadily led her back to stand before him, an inches breath between their chests, yet they didn't touch.

"I will come with you."

Her voice was strong, and Rajsa let out a long sigh. Sade reached up on her toes and kissed him quietly on the lips.

Chapter 28

Kana was sitting on the top step of her vardo, and she looked up as they approached. She saw the pang of bitterness that passed in her eyes before being hidden under a hooded expression.

"Kana—this is Rajsa," Sade said softly, looking into her sister's eyes and begging for her to understand.

Kana stood up, walked down the steps to stand before them. She said nothing for a long moment, looking at Rajsa. Then she turned to Sade, her hand reaching out for hers. Though no words passed between them, they both knew that this was the moment of their parting.

"I should have known that you were too good to be true," she said, slowly shaking her head.

"I am sorry, Kana," Sade whispered, falling into her sister's arms.

"Some things aren't meant to be."

The words sounded so sorrowful, coming from her lips, and Sade began to cry. Kana pulled away, hiding the tears in her eyes. She handed Sade her pack, and Sade realized that she had known from the moment Rajsa arrived that she would be leaving.

"Take good care of my sister," she said to Rajsa.

His arm crept around her. "I will."

Kana gazed at Sade with a sad smile. "Maybe at Bromberg we will meet again."

Sade laughed softly and looked at the ground. "Maybe. I will look for you."

"Goodbye, Sade."

Sade spoke little as Rajsa led her back to his kumpania. He carried Sade's bag slung over his shoulder, and his other hand rested on the small of her back.

Her head was bent, her shoulders slumped. Inky blackness swirled in the pit of her stomach, and she wondered if she had been right to leave her sister behind.

Rajsa leaned over her, planting a soft kiss on the top of her brow. She sighed, resting her head momentarily on his shoulder.

Dusk had long since fallen when they reached the place where they had camped, alight with the small cooking fires that glowed in the night. As they came around the side of Esmae's vardo, there was sudden commotion as she and Vento jumped away from each other. Esmae's eyes landed on Sade in surprise, and she looked questioningly between her and Rajsa.

"Sade is coming with us," Rajsa said quietly, sitting down on the ground.

Cautiously, Vento sat down too, drawing Esmae down beside him. There was no stirring in the rest of the camp.

"So—" Esmae still had questions in her eyes.

Sade smiled to herself, ducking her head as Rajsa's hand found hers. When she looked up again, she saw Esmae grinning with a knowing look in her eyes. She shook her head and leaned on Vento's shoulder.

"Vento and I, too," she whispered.

Silence fell between them as they watched the flames burn down. The full moon shown down from the starry sky, and it had well crossed its path before they bade each other goodnight and crept under thick layers of covers.

Chapter 29

In the early light of dawn, Sade stood before the mirror in Esmae's caravan, plaiting her hair over her shoulder. When she was done, she stepped back and looked at herself. She was wearing a brown shirt under Esmae's greenish coat, and a long blue skirt. With Kana's scarf in her hair, she thought she looked like a true Romani, and no longer the forlorn girl she had left behind.

Raised voices reached her ears, and she peered out of the foggy window. The blurred shapes of two men appeared in the glass, and she cracked open the door and looked out.

Jamal was pounding his fist in the air, pointing at Rajsa.

"You are a fool!" He cried. "Don't shame us by bringing her back here. She is no more than a Gadze in disguise; she misleads you!"

Sade flinched at his words.

Rajsa bent his head under the blows, but said nothing. Jamal strode forward and grabbed the lapels of his jacket, jerking Rajsa until he was looking at him.

"Do you hear what I'm saying, boy? Marry her and you will be banned."

The sentence hung in the air like a knife poised to strike. Jamal spat in Rajsa's face and turned away, glaring at the other Romani. Sade gulped and closed the door, turning away.

Moments later, she heard footsteps come up the stairs. She turned away when Rajsa entered; pretended to be examining a shirt. He stopped behind her, his presence heavy in the space.

She tipped her chin to her shoulder. "I will leave."

"No!" There was defiance in his voice. "I don't care what Jamal says."

"I won't let you shame your people." Her words forced tears into her eyes, but she bit them back.

Rajsa's hand was on her shoulder. "Our people are falling apart, Sade. Jamal tries to hide it, but it is in the eyes of the people; we all know it." His gentle hands turned her to face him. "I love you, Sade, and no rules of the world will change that."

"I love you, too, Rajsa," she whispered, running a finger along the edge of his neckline. "But you shouldn't fight among yourselves. Somehow I thought that it would change how Jamal looked at me, but I was wrong." She pushed past him.

"Wait." He grabbed her arm. "You want to leave?"

"I can't stand being the subject of his wrath anymore, Rajsa."

"Then I will come with you. We will go south; start a kumpania of our own. Maybe Vento and Esmae will come with us." He drew her near, kissed her forehead. "Please, Sade?"

Sade raised her eyes to his, softly shaking her head.

"You are a wild Gypsy man, Rajsa," she whispered.

Epilogue

It was a sad parting, between them and the other Romani. Esmae and Vento decided to come with them, and everyone couldn't help but feeling that the Romani tradition was slowly falling apart.

Sade sat on the steps of Esmae's vardo, waiting. The women were crowded around Esmae, showering her with gifts and kisses. The men were more modest, patting each other on their back as they solemnly bade each other farewell.

Rajsa came to stand beside her, raising his eyes to her face. "Are you ready to go?"

"As ready as I'll ever be."

He smiled, and Sade grinned back, kissing him. She slipped an arm around his shoulders and rested her head on his chest.

"Sade!"

They both turned, and saw Jamal standing off in the shadows, his gray eyes clouded in the morning light. Sade gulped as he beckoned to her, and Rajsa's hand tightened in hers.

"What do you want, Jamal?" He asked.

"Just a word, with Sade."

She glanced at Rajsa, unsure, but slowly he nodded for her to go. Cautiously, she slipped down the steps and drew up to the old man. For a moment she stood there, not daring to look into his face, her heart thumping in her chest.

"I'm sorry I was angry with you," he said.

Sade looked up in shock.

Jamal's face was hard set, but there was a foreign look of softness in his eyes. His voice grated like rough stones as he went on.

"Don't think that I don't hate you and your people, or that I don't believe that you brought the Gadze to Bromberg. Only—" His voice softened. "You remind me of a daughter I once had, and from the first moment I saw you I couldn't help but think you could have been my own."

His eyes turned to stone as Sade opened her mouth to speak.

"Don't go on thinking I will shower you with love like the rest of those gaudy women. I am just trying to say I'm sorry for what I've said, and, and—" He faltered. "I don't want you thinking of me like a bitter old man."

Sade stood in stunned silence. "You mean—"

Jamal's nostrils flared, and he suddenly growled. "I mean nothing." He turned half way away from her. "I never should have said anything."

"Wait." Sade tentatively touched his arm, her heart suddenly overflowing for this confused man. "It's okay, Jamal. Don't be ashamed."

He glared at her. "I am *not* ashamed." He waved an angry hand. "Go; go with your lover man. Get away from this dying kumpania."

"I—" Sade took a step back, gripping her skirts.

"Go!" His voice was rising. Sade stepped back a couple more feet, and then turned away.

"Don't tell them what I said."

She hesitated. He stood with his familiar scowl on his face, but his eyes were pleading. She nodded, barely, and went on walking.

Rajsa was watching her as she came back. "What did he say?"

Sade shook her head, glancing at Jamal. "I'm not sure. But it is nothing." She looked away from the old man and smiled.

Rajsa raised an eyebrow, but the shrugged his shoulders. "It is time to go."

He scooped up Jonah, and helped Sade into the vardo. Esmae climbed up beside them, her hands brushing past the lingering touches of her friends. There were tears in her eyes, but there was a smile on her face as she looked at Sade and Jonah.

Vento took the reins, Rajsa climbing up beside him, and with a click from his tongue the caravan lurched forward. Sade raised her hand in farewell, and beyond the group of Romani she saw a lone man raise his hand in return.

Jonah slipped her hand into Sade's as they watched the kumpania melt away into the trees behind them.

"I'm glad you came back, Sade," she said.

Sade kissed the top of her head, tenderness glowing in her heart for this child. "Even if it means that we are leaving the rest of the Romani behind?"

"Even if we are leaving them." She looked up at Sade with a perplexed look on her face. "Are you like my Moma now, Sade?"

Sade laughed softly, leaning her head against the wood. "I suppose, in some ways."

Jonah grinned, laying her face in her lap. "I think you are. And now we are going on an adventure." The child rambled on, and over her head Sade looked at Esmae and smiled.

"We've always been on an adventure," she whispered softly.

Made in the USA
San Bernardino, CA
07 May 2017